ROGUE PLANET

STEVEN M. MOORE

Rogue Planet

Steven M. Moore

Copyright Steven M. Moore 2016

Carrick Publishing

Original Cover Art by Sara Carrick
ISBN Kindle, 978-1-77242-033-3
ISBN e-Pub, 978-1-77242-035-7
ISBN Print, 978-1-77242-036-4

Praise for Steven M. Moore's SciFi novels:

The Midas Bomb: "Castilblanco engages the world beyond his cases…. Bravo to *The Midas Bomb*: Its explosion certainly has my attention!"—White Cat

Angels Need Not Apply: "This book is just plain awesome!"—Dave

Teeter-Totter between Lust and Murder: "A tightly written political thriller with lots of twists and turns."—Duncan

Aristocrats and Assassins: "…a textbook example of a self-contained story that is part of a series…leaves the audience, satisfied, fulfilled, and looking forward to the next big adventure."—GoodBadBizarre

The Collector: "Art theft and child sexual abuse…. *The Collector* has successfully merged these two criminal activities to create the latest in the NYPD homicide detectives Chen and Castilblanco series."—Bookbuzz

*The first edition of *The Midas Bomb* is still available as a trade paperback. All other books are e-books.

Survivors of the Chaos: "…Moore has a way of describing his characters that really makes them come to life…. Through some pretty varied characters, you get to see the vast and detailed setting that the author envisioned, sometimes through some pretty unexpected plot twists."—Kellie Sheridan, Sift Book Reviews

More than Human: The Mensa Contagion: "…kept me turning pages after I should have put the book down…. I found the characters well developed and the plot fresh. I was reminded of Kim Stanley Robinson's Mars trilogy."—Debra Miller, Amazon reviewer

Dedication

In memory of John G. Stockmyer, who showed it
could be done.

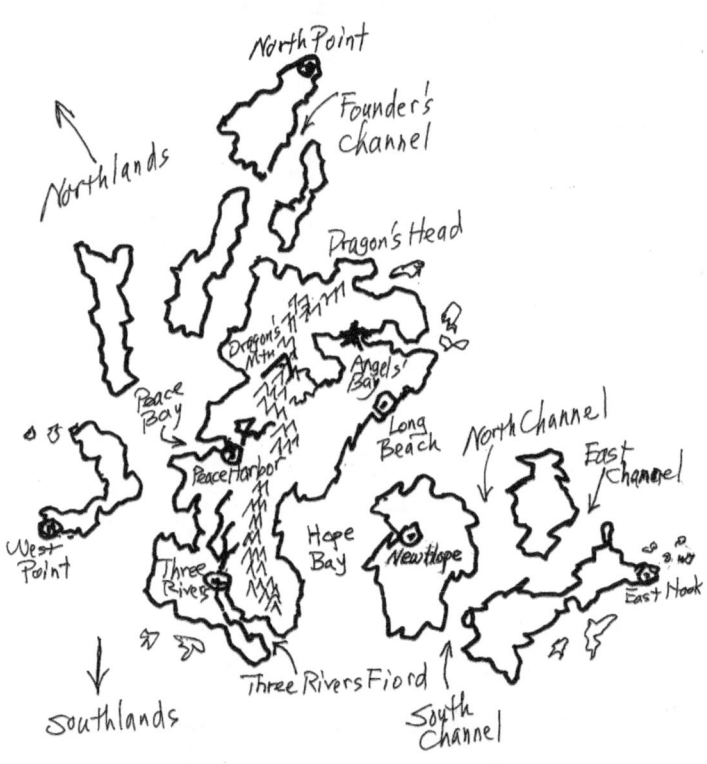

EDEN'S BIG ISLAND & VICINITY

Cast of Main Characters

Gol Kovlyn = First Tribe's First Pilgrim and King Breman's High Priest and Magician

The Founder = religious leader who led the faithful to settle both Paradise and Eden

King Breman = First Tribe's king

King Merson = Kaushal's father and Second Tribe's king

Mela = Kaushal's mother and King Merson's first wife

Kaushal = Second Tribe prince, son of King Merson and Mela

Anju = First Tribe princess

Kifi = a leader of the Mountain Folk

Tristan = another leader of the Mountain Folk and Guide to the Way

Ezan = another Mountain Folk woman

Petro, Samos, and Kindri = Wilders leaders

King Farben = King Breman's replacement

Rezo Banton = captain of the Zheng He, an ITUIP explorer ship

Mera Deeson = a Human lawyer who aids Kaushal on New Haven

Kiana = Kaushal's collaborator for returning to Eden

Pel = "The General" and another Kaushal collaborator

Part One

From Paradise to Eden

Hidden away from near-Earth planets in remote spiral arms of the Galaxy are Human worlds that have lost contact with more progressive worlds and reverted to strange and primitive customs and traditions, their leaders using religion, superstition, and imported technologies to rule in tyranny. Explorer and survey ships from ITUIP (Interstellar Trade Union of Independent Planets) catalogued these planets as suitable for future colonization centuries earlier, but groups with a special interest in ensuring a homogeneous and often despotic society didn't bother applying for permission to colonize. Following the ITUIP Protocol, ships were restricted to observe and maintain a hands-off policy, even when there was a great temptation to intervene. These planets are often called rogue planets....

—Swims-in-Rapids, University of New Haven Professor of Sociology (translated from buzzspeak)

Chapter One

Paradise

Gol Kovlyn turned away from the window, tired of watching snow fall. The window was wasted because frozen ocean, huge drifts, and growing glaciers comprised the vista. His world was dying and his people were starving. Millions of bodies were already stacked into ice caves, too many to bury. Only a privileged few had enough food and heat.

The First Tribe had arrived at this world only three centuries earlier, a world already possessing harsh winters due to its axis tilt, but they prospered until their star started to fade. "A natural cycle," the scientists said. "A curse for our sins," he had argued. Neither was right. They'd hastened another ice age because pollution from their antiquated industries had hastened the extreme weather. Summers were warmer, but the land area too insignificant to mitigate the effect of cooling oceans. Paradise, once a water world with some archipelagoes, had become an ice world.

Age-wise he would be in his prime but for a bad diet and lack of exercise. He didn't go outside much, even before the ice age, and often would have late meals with abundant drink relaxing after his late night trysts. He had more stamina than his partners of late. They were attractive and young, but they were also hungry because they were chosen from the children of the poor. Kovlyn didn't waste much food on them either. The Founder had always said the poor were assured a special place alongside the Almighty Ra. Kovlyn didn't see any problem with hastening that blissful journey.

He walked to his ornate desk and sat in the matching, high-backed chair. The desk's front had human hands carved into the wood; those cupped hands held their world. Most people knew there were other worlds, but it was blasphemy to talk about them. These were the hands of the Almighty Amun-Ra comforting His people. They needed a lot of comforting now, these poor wretches destined for eternal bliss.

Few trading ships visited the planet. Those that did were often looking for rare earth ores in exchange for high tech products. Upper echelons, nobles and priests anointed by the Almighty Ra and His son and daughter, Isis and Osiris, were able to maintain some semblance of a technological society that way, but most of the faithful lived at a subsistence level, especially now, clinging to their belief their time here was a brief moment on the road to eternal life in the arms of the Founder.

Hanging across from him was the portrait of that holy man, but it only displayed the back of his head. The long, black mane of hair was streaked with gray. Only Kovlyn, the First Pilgrim, could visit the tomb to gaze upon the face of the embalmed man. The Founder was the original First Pilgrim; in contrast to Kovlyn, he was a man with a thin face, sunken cheeks, and wild eyes framed by bushy eyebrows. Kovlyn always thought it was a bit much to execute anyone who tried to draw that face, but he kept those thoughts to himself. The regime applied the same punishment to those who blasphemed the Almighty Ra and the great Isis and Osiris.

The Founder was a man who became a god. Every First Pilgrim since his demise was considered more than Human—the incarnation of the Almighty Ra, Isis, and Osiris in living flesh. No one dared question that logic, especially not Kovlyn, of course. Everyone knew belief and logic were one and the same when it came to the Almighty Ra.

The Founder's story wasn't common knowledge. Only priests knew the details. And only the First Pilgrim knew the Founder's name. As a teen, the Founder had worked on a dairy farm on a planet light years away. He had ventured into an open field one day when a storm blew in. Struck by lightning, his parents found him drooling and babbling about his vision of the Almighty Ra. The deity told the Founder to spread his story first and then take his followers to establish two colonies where they could worship the Almighty Ra in peace and reverence. One colony was for Isis, the other for Osiris. Two corresponding tribes were formed. Somehow they lost track of which colony corresponded to which offspring. The colonized planets were called Paradise and Eden.

Those beliefs didn't inhibit the intrigue among nobles and priests. Assassinations were common and punishment for assassinations rare as the assassin assumed control. The first and best advice he'd received when he was passed the Golden Scimitar, the avenging weapon of the First Pilgrim, was to watch his back. He always did. It would be unusual for a noble or priest to go after him. As the king's Mage, he was considered all powerful, so they all expected such action was doomed to fail. He made sure they continued to think that way.

One floor of one tower of the Almighty Ra's Spiritual Center provided him with quarters, office, and chapel, a tower taller than any of the nobility's royal palaces and only meters shorter than the castle of King Breman. His heart was heavy, though, in spite of his exalted place in Paradise society. He was the spiritual leader and Grand Magician of the world, but now he had some doubts. *Have I failed the Almighty Amun-Ra and not protected his children?*

A knock at the office door interrupted his thoughts. "Enter."

***

A messenger entered, gave the usual fist-to-heart salute, and bowed. "First Pilgrim Kovlyn, the Second Tribe has answered your plea for assistance." He handed Kovlyn a message tablet. As usual for Royal Messengers, this one wasn't much older than a young street urchin, but he wore the uniform of the Palace Guards, carrying both a pistol and long sword. His faded purple cape bore the same symbolic hands and world as Kovlyn's desk front.

First Pilgrim was his official title, although everyone and anyone could be called Pilgrim on Paradise. In their language, a special ending on the word implied he was the most important Pilgrim, so the word First was implied. He had first options on technology acquired from visiting merchants, so he was also called the King's Mage. The poor believed in magic, so they interpreted all technology as magic originating with him.

He stood and paced the floor, hands clasped behind his back, holding the tablet. *The Second Tribe's planet is the only solution!* The intense man, his baldness hidden by the dark purple biretta matching the color of his robe and pointed slippers, was nobody's fool. He knew the Second Tribe's king would exact many favors for saving the First Tribe. The man was a shrewd ruler. Kovlyn was afraid to read the message.

He passed near the messenger and wrinkled his nose. The messenger's bathing habits weren't uncommon among the poor, but the man-boy also reeked of cheap liquor. Both hands were missing fingers, probably victims to frostbite. *A local. Is such a lout even worth saving?* No Royal Guards should visit the First Pilgrim in such a condition!

Nevertheless, he gave the young soldier a coin and then waved his hand over the tablet, his large ring's emissions bringing it to life. He recognized the speaker as His Highness Hach Merson, the Second Tribe's king.

"I have met with our Council and we have decided to accept the First Tribe's survivors as refugees." *Refugees? We're the First Tribe, the Founder's chosen. The impudent bastard!* "We are sending twenty ships with minimal crews so we can save as many of you as possible. We'll have room for about forty thousand people. It will be crowded, and some might not survive the journey. I recommend leaving the weak, infirm, elderly, and very young children behind, but that's your decision, of course. Ships will be orbiting Paradise in three days, the Almighty Ra willing."

Forty thousand? That was better than he'd expected. He could increase the number in his list by twenty per cent. Heretics would be left behind too, of course, as well as Outlanders who hid in far-away archipelagoes to escape his king's rule. They might hear about the coming ships—they had extensive spy networks—and walk en masse across frozen seas, but the true faithful would be gone by the time they arrived.

"I'll journey to the Royal Chambers and inform King Breman," Kovlyn said. "We need a royal decree."

The king was often in a drunken stupor but had his uses. Kovlyn was the man in charge. *As the Almighty Ra and the Founder intended.*

***

One immediate organizational problem was to clear a landing zone in the old spaceport for twenty starships from the Second Tribe. Kovlyn suggested a solution and King Breman signed off on it—he had no choice.

Around the spaceport shanty towns had sprouted. Hovels there offered some protection from cold and storms. The birthrate among the poor was so high, though, it didn't matter how many died. And a hovel didn't stay empty for long. The poor toiled at menial jobs. Lucky ones were stevedores used to unload trade ships that visited the ice planet and dared to land in the worst conditions any of them would ever see.

Kovlyn's suggestion was simple: take back some of the land used by squatters. Those who resisted would be killed or driven onto the sea ice to freeze. Most wouldn't be going to the Second Tribe's planet anyway.

He had needed to swallow his pride when he groveled to King Merson. *He took long enough to make his decision!* The First Tribe's ships were non-functional FTL ships dating back to the days when the Founder had led his people to Eden and Paradise. Elsewhere they had been decommissioned and replaced. Without the climate crisis, they would never have needed ships.

Generations ago, another First Pilgrim had written an edict—visiting merchant ships would be allowed to land and take off, but the First Tribe's fleet wouldn't be replaced. *Maybe that hadn't been wise.* He savored the blasphemous thought. He was in charge now. He defined what was sanctioned and what was heretical.

***

Kovlyn had heard Eden was tropical. He hugged himself against Paradise's cold, watching Royal Guards go about their grisly business. A wave of his finger brought one to him running.

"Yes, First Pilgrim?"

"I tire of seeing those poor devils turned into seared meat. Try to herd as many squatters as possible onto the ice. Let the cold kill them. There'll be less cleanup that way. And frozen bodies don't stink."

The Guard ran off to carry out his orders.

Where was I? Eden. What do I know about it? An insignificant axis tilt made for a nearly constant climate that only varied with altitude, a positive, but it too was a water world. Yet there were large land masses in many archipelagoes. *All good compared to our home world.*

He knew peasants from his world would adapt well and fit into the agrarian society of their new home. That could be a problem. *We need to maintain control of our own and not associate too much with the Second Tribe's devils.*

He had an idea: he would convince the Second Tribe that the First Tribe's survivors should be quarantined on some remote archipelago where there weren't many natives, if any. *We need to invent some kind of disease.* As First Pilgrim, he had access to some old databases. He would choose a disease that didn't show many external symptoms but was reputed to be contagious. *That will put the fear of the Almighty Amun-Ra in the leaders of the Second Tribe!*

***

"First Pilgrim, the fleet commander is waiting for an audience," said the messenger.

"Show him in," said Kovlyn.

The bow was deep. He liked that. "First Pilgrim, as representative of our mighty King Merson, I salute you." The fleet commander, who was dressed in thick clothing and a fur cap, clicked the heels of his boots together and put two fingers of his right hand to his brow. *What's that about?* "We are ready to begin evacuation upon your orders."

"Of course. For appearances, nobles will be the last to board, and I will follow them. But I have a warning for you and crews from your ships."

"A warning?" said the man, who frowned and raised his bushy eyebrows.

"Don't worry. It isn't much of a problem. We are now fighting a little epidemic. Something called Johnson Pox brought on by our unsanitary conditions at this vexing time. The nobles are healthy, but many others might be sick or about to be. When we arrive on Eden, is there anywhere you can quarantine us for a while?"

The commander nodded. "Already planned. We have removed a small number of peasants who were farming a few small tracts of land on a remote archipelago. We thought you might prefer land of your own, at least until you can integrate into our society. I wouldn't call that original plan a quarantine, but we can make it so." He pointed to his nose. "We came prepared with filters." He smiled. "You never know what you might run across on other planets."

Nose filters? What about mouth filters? But the First Pilgrim had noted the man hadn't opened his mouth. Words were emitted from a device on his chest. There was also a device implanted behind his right ear. *They have more technology!* Kovlyn had seen merchants with these implants.

He decided he shouldn't be surprised at that. The Second Tribe had a small merchant fleet, after all. *These are blasphemers! Second Tribe indeed!*

Chapter Two

Eden

"How goes the invasion?" said the First Pilgrim.

The quarantine was over. It had given Breman and Kovlyn enough time to organize against the Second Tribe's King Merson. King Breman stayed sober long enough to exhibit some skill as a strategist.

The First Pilgrim had decided Merson's forces were complacent and lazy. They also seemed to expect the First Tribe to be forever grateful about being offered refuge on Eden. *The Founder's strength flows in us; Merson and his soldiers are weak.*

The Royal Guard bowed again. "Very well, sir. They are running from us, leaving good equipment behind, as you predicted. They must know they're outnumbered, but the Second Tribe doesn't know how to fight either."

"That's because the Second Tribe isn't the Almighty Ra's favorite. Their gods are greed, money, and power. Our revolution is a righteous one."

The field commander looked puzzled. *Does he think they're my gods too?* He mentally shrugged. It didn't matter. The man was a fool who would die for the Founder and his representatives on Eden, the First Pilgrim and King Breman.

"How do we proceed, sir?"

"Chase the heretics into the ocean. They will come back with their ships, and we will be ready to take on those too."

"What if they attack us from above? They have spaceships too."

Kovlyn smiled. *I like this fellow! He's clever.* "That's taken care of. Let's say your troops won't have to worry about their spaceships. Merchant ships will be worthless to them too, and there aren't many others that are armed. King Merson is a peaceful man, you know. Too bad he'll soon be dead."

After the soldier left, Kovlyn sat at his new desk, a simple table First Tribe members had left behind years ago when they'd arrived and gone into quarantine. The separation between First and Second Tribe had guaranteed the First had time to plot and prepare.

We are going to take over this world in the name of the Almighty Ra!

***

King Merson looked upon his court with sadness. He hated war, but there was no doubt now that the Second Tribe was at war with the First. His mission of mercy to save them had made them bitter, envious, and jealous. *Or, is it their First Pilgrim's ambitions?* He feared he'd never know.

He jumped at the sound as another captured spaceship was destroyed not far away. The boom rocked the castle. Most of his troops had fled the spaceport days ago and likely were already into the mountains towering in the center of Big Island. *I should have sent the First Tribe to those snow-covered peaks! We could have kept a watch on them and confined them there.*

He wasn't a strong man—more philosopher than fighter. His brown, curly locks were awry now, and he had no idea the crown sat askew on his head. His eyes, the color of Eden's seas, were moist with emotion. He clasped his hands in front of him, feeling their clamminess. *My time is short.*

The Second Tribe had elected not to stay on Paradise and went on to Eden. Now he was about to lose the planet to the First Tribe. The Second Tribe's High Priest, Gol Kovlyn's equivalent, had been burned at the stake as a heretic. Others from their clergy had fled either to the mountains or Southlands. The planet was in chaos.

Five wives and a dozen children waited for him to speak. They were on their knees, foreheads on the ground, in deference to their monarch. He'd never approved of such fawning—indeed, he usually insisted on a simple bow, but they were family. *His family!*

"Please, all rise." He waited. Some children helped their mothers to their feet. "War is upon us, and it's not going well. We have already lost the spaceport and most of the city. Our priests are gone so no last rites will be said and no funerals according to our traditions will occur. We have offered to surrender, but the First Tribe has refused to negotiate." The king sighed. He had failed them. "We originally came here to live in peace, and now we're at war with those who we aided. I shouldn't have been so naive. I should have been more careful." Some seemed surprised at that admission. Public opinion had come down hard against the First Tribe and its leaders. *But I have failed!* "A squadron composed of my most elite Royal Guards will guarantee your safe passage into the foothills. Some here know there are many caves there. You will be safe and be able to live off the land until this war is finished. Take only essentials with you. My men will help you carry your items and the smaller children. My love goes with you."

No time to become emotional, he thought, walking through the door to the right and in back of the throne into his private chambers. But he expected the worst consequences. His people hadn't been prepared for war. *And that's on me.*

***

"Mama, why is it so cold?"

Mela rubbed her son's arms. "Would you throw another stick on the fire, Benish?"

The old Guard nodded. There was plenty of wood, but the cave's damp air made cold the victor over heat from all but the largest bonfire. He empathized with the royal lady and her brood.

"Shall I explain, ma'am, the idea of altitude? Kaushal is a curious lad."

He admired this woman. They had all been through hell, but her pleasant disposition still survived. Stress and bad food had left her and her children looking frail, though. Her will to persevere and her love for her children made the small, auburn-haired woman a saint in his eyes. *Damn the First Tribe!*

She hugged the waif, who now looked more like a peasant than royalty. Benish preferred to keep it that way to protect the child. Anyone looking upon those brown, curly locks and bright, blue eyes might see the old king in his son, but the disguise would have to do.

"Please do so. I have to look after his sisters and brothers." She stood and retreated farther into the cave.

"Altitude measures height," said Kaushal, who stood with his hands on his hips, looking up at Benish with a stern expression and bright eyes.

"Very good," said their bodyguard with a laugh. "More precisely, altitude is height. Starships fly at tremendous heights, coming from and going to the stars."

"Have you seen other stars?"

Benish ruffled the boy's curls. "Long ago. We came from there. You know the stories about the Tribes. And I once served as security on a merchant ship." He pointed to the cave's mouth and upwards. "There are many intelligent beings in just our galaxy, and not just Humans. In known space, there are billions, and that's only a small fraction of our galaxy. There are also many galaxies. Billions of them. It's awe-inspiring."

"I know some of that. But why am I cold?"

"It is hot below, and hot during the day and cold at night here, because, in general, temperature decreases with altitude and the thinner air radiates heat faster at night. Water boils at higher altitude too. Here on Eden, altitude is everything. But here in the caves, it's always cold. Other planets' temperature variations can depend more on the tilt of their axes relative to the parent star. Think of a big ball spinning. There are two points that don't move, and the line between them is the axis. How that line is oriented relative to the motion of the planet around its star can produce severe climatic effects. Do you understand?"

"Some. I'd prefer a ball to play with. We left all my toys."

"I'm sorry about that," said Benish, "but we could only carry so much."

"I know. Someday I will return and kill all the First Tribe."

"Some might consider that justice." *For example, me.* "But the First Tribe isn't responsible. Their leaders are. They lost their planet and now want ours. It's that simple."

"I see nothing simple about it. There's plenty of land on Eden. We could have shared."

Benish studied the child. *Wisdom can come from the mouths of babes. Why don't we heed them more often?*

***

Three months later the First Tribe's soldiers found them, gaunt and hungry. Others had fled to even higher ground. Kaushal's mother, Mela, didn't have the strength, nor did his younger siblings. Benish had stayed behind to protect them.

Kaushal cowered far back in the cave. He had run ahead when the guns had killed his mother and Benish as they tried to tuck his brothers and sisters into crevices where they would be safe from the invaders. Their anguished cries had ended in a foreboding silence. Frozen in fear, he was ready to meet the Almighty Ra, although he couldn't understand why He had deserted his family or why He had chosen sides with such villains.

Kaushal was shaking when they found him.

"Come out, boy," said the soldier, reaching into the small recess. "No one's going to hurt you."

Kaushal knew better. He had heard the end of his siblings' cries. Other soldiers snickered. He heard one hack up phlegm and spit.

"Damn it, it's cold in here. We should blast the whore's son and be done with it."

"We can't kill every member of the Second Tribe," said the first soldier. "Who would be our slaves? Pabi, you're small enough to crawl in there and bring the whelp out."

Pabi, not much bigger than Kaushal, crawled in and grabbed the boy's arm, only to be bitten. He punched the kid, who screamed in pain but then feigned unconsciousness.

"You didn't damage him, did you?" said the first soldier.

The man called Pabi pulled Kaushal out by his arms. He was hoping to make a run for it, sure he could beat them to the mouth of the cave. Where he'd go after that was another question.

"He's fine," said Pabi. "Can't take a punch, that's all. Like all these Eden folk. Soft and weak. Too bad we didn't have a chance at the woman. She's a looker."

They all nodded.

"We could have taken turns," said the spitter—Kaushal recognized his voice. "Now we can bugger this lad, Pilgrim."

"Stow it," said the first soldier. "Only heretics practice sodomy, you ass. If you don't do it like a real man, you'll be damned. The First Pilgrim often preaches against such deviant behavior. What's the matter with you?"

"So, what do we do with him?"

"Clean him up and sell him, what else? The rich always need servants. He's the last one alive. The cave will be the others' tomb. The ground's too frozen to bury them. Bugs will have them for their spring repasts." He spat too. "I need to leave these damned mountains. Bring him along now."

Chapter Three

The Slave

They pushed Kaushal, in handcuffs and shackles with a leash around his neck, onto the auction block. He was naked, but he was clean and well fed, now the picture of good health. He rubbed the socket behind his ear. The old woman who scrubbed him had ripped out the com device. Its batteries had died months ago. His head still rang at times— the harridan hadn't been gentle. But he was the first one to admit he'd needed a bath.

The bidding started. At first, there were multiple bidders, but a murmur then went through the crowd. Bidding had stopped when an older man in front nodded.

"You're a lucky boy," said the auctioneer, his voice a whisper in Kaushal's good ear. "That's King Breman's representative. You're going to be living with royalty, my little friend."

Kaushal frowned. He had no desire to live with royalty, not when it involved the First Tribe. He'd kill them all if he could. But maybe he would now have a chance to do that!

His work as a slave started in the huge kitchens used to prepare food for the king and his court. Any mistake he made brought the wrath of a cook down upon him, usually in the form of a beating with any handy wooden ladle. Once scalding water was tossed his way, but he ducked in time. He learned, and, in learning, survived.

Two weeks after his birthday (only he remembered, of course), the sous-chef caught him humming. She smiled at him.

She was as wide as she was tall—Kaushal already was taller—but she always maintained a good humor in spite of the drudgery in her life. She had also reprimanded the lower-ranked chef who had tossed water at Kaushal. The words she had used were new ones for Kaushal. He filed them away for future use.

"Learn some First Tribe songs, Kaushal, and you can become an entertainer." She made upward motions with her hands as if she were savoring vapors emanating from a stew. "You have a good voice, lad. One must always use the natural gifts the Almighty Amun-Ra gives us."

Alone that night in the dormitory where he slept with other single male Second Tribe slaves, Kaushal thought about that. *Do I have a good voice?* His mother had been musical. She had managed to sing for the children when they were living in that mountain cave. Before the First Tribe appeared on the scene, he had heard rumors about how her musical gifts enchanted his father. *I'd prefer to be a slave who entertains than a slave who takes out the garbage and lifts heavy pots.*

How do I learn First Tribe music? Do they even have music? He knew most entertainment was considered an insult to the Founder. Second Tribe entertainers were among the earliest beheaded. The First Pilgrim was strict about what music the Almighty Ra allowed. Kaushal rubbed his neck. He'd also prefer to take out garbage than lose his head. *I have to stay alive long enough to avenge my mother and father.*

But if I'm careful and focus on First Tribe songs? He already knew how to play the roki a bit, a four-stringed instrument. His mother had sung to his simple chordal accompaniment. He decided to learn to play solos. He also learned some First Tribe songs, what they called "legend songs," musical sagas celebrating the Almighty Ra, Isis, Osiris, and the Founder's leading them to Paradise. The sagas were stupid and inaccurate if the history of the two tribes he knew were true, but the music could be sweet or warlike, depending on the story. *If I ignore the words, I can stomach this. The music's OK.*

***

"What are they doing?" said Kaushal, looking over the girl's shoulder.

She turned and smiled at him. He fell to his knees and bowed to her.

"Please pardon me, my princess, for I knew not who you were."

He had seen her in the castle before but only from a distance, yet he had recognized Princess Anju. She was about his height, a young girl who was becoming a woman. He had managed only a brief glimpse of her eyes, but they were enchanting. *So full of life!*

She put a finger to her lips. "Get up, you fool, and be quiet. I'm not supposed to be here. I wanted to see."

He stood, his eyes still focused on the floor. "See what? What's going on?"

"Three more beheadings," she said in a whisper. "These are artists from your tribe who dared paint caricatures of the Founder's face as a protest. I want to see if Wilders save them."

"Beheadings?" Kaushal trembled but swallowed his fear. Even that kind of violent death might be preferred to his present state of slavery. His body ached from his most recent beating by the main chef.

"The First Pilgrim rarely offers clemency," she said. "He had the arms cut off one of our own people for stealing bread from the royal kitchens. Considering the thief was a cook, that punishment condemns him to a life of begging."

Kaushal shuddered again. *So that's where his friend had gone!* That friend had often given him tasty leftovers from palace feasts. This First Pilgrim would be the first member of the First Tribe he'd kill if he had the chance.

"Who are the Wilders?"

She turned to him, astonishment on her face. Even that expression was attractive. He was mesmerized. He scanned her blossoming body in a heartbeat, and she blushed but smiled at him.

"You're not up on current events, are you? Wilders are marauders from the Second Tribe who are burning and pillaging our peasant people's villages and farmlands in the southern provinces. They've been known to come here and save people from execution. I thought that would be exciting to watch." She winked. "They say Wilders men are strong and make great lovers."

Was she implying he was weak and wouldn't be a good lover? He decided to ignore the comment. "Do you want Wilders to stop these beheadings?"

Again the finger to the lips. "I hate killings and executions," she said in a whisper again, nodding. "Long ago, back on Paradise, my uncle, the current king, killed my father, who was king. I'm betrothed to my uncle now. I pray every day that Wilders kill him."

"I'm surprised this First Pilgrim permits incest. Isn't it taboo?"

"He doesn't. The king is my stepmother's brother. It's complicated."

He nodded. He remembered the Second Tribe's court as being complicated too. *So long ago. I wonder what happened to all of them.* He only knew what happened to his mother and siblings.

Wilders didn't appear, and the beheadings took place. Kaushal watched the heads roll and blood flow. *No, I prefer to die a slave.* Anju squeezed his hand.

"I have to go," the princess said, tears in her eyes. She dashed off.

Kaushal appreciated her discomfort. He vomited into a flower pot. The flowers were already withered and dry from watching too much death.

Chapter Four

The Entertainer

Two weeks later, Kaushal wound through a maze of corridors and tunnels, many underground, and found a secluded and breezy courtyard he remembered from his childhood in the castle. The walls were high enough to trap most sounds he made practicing the roki, and lush vegetation muted the echoes. He knew several places like this, and rotated between them, randomizing his choices to avoid discovery.

He only stopped playing and singing when he saw the shadow cast on the stone floor. When she peeked around the corner of the column, he smiled at Princess Anju.

"Will you report me?"

She stepped from behind the column. "No, as long as you don't report me."

"Agreed. Are you in trouble?"

"My uncle would go into a fit of rage if he knew I'm alone with a Second Tribe slave. He might kill me even, like he did my father. And he'd likely kill you too. Or, at the very least, castrate you."

"I suppose my voice would turn to soprano in that case," he said with a smile. He had no idea where he'd heard that. *Was it the practice in his father's court?* Even the Second Tribe frowned on female singers, so boys and men singing countertenor took their place. *Maybe they weren't countertenors to begin with?*

"That's not funny," she said. She sat on the opposite end of the bench, folding her hands in her lap. "Can I listen to more?"

"You make me nervous," he said.

"A performer with no audience is a hibjab shrieking at the moon."

"What's a hibjab?"

"Some animal on Paradise, I suppose, before the Ice Age. It's just a saying. It means—"

He held up a hand. "I figured out what it means. You're saying I should practice with an audience, and you'll be my first audience member."

She nodded. "Please, continue."

She listened to him for a while and then stood.

"I have to go. Do you often come here? I only found this place today."

"There are many secret spots like this in the castle. I can show you if you like."

She raised an eyebrow but followed with a smile. "I'd like that."

***

"You didn't!"

"People in the court will love your songs and playing," said Princess Anju.

"I don't want to entertain the court. Why should I? You people have taken over my world."

She frowned. "Not I. And don't be so stubborn. Other Second Tribe slaves are courtiers. It's a privilege and an escape from a hard life." She put her tiny hand on his arm. "Do it for me."

He looked at her long hair, longing to touch it. Her cloak and dress hid her youthful figure, but not from his imagination. This girl was an angel. He smiled. *Maybe the*

24

capital city and huge inlet from the sea, Angels' Bay, is named for her and her kindred souls? But a sour taste filled his mouth. *Those would be the Founder's angels!* He equated those with demons.

"Maybe. Let me think about it."

Kaushal was already wondering if being a court entertainer might allow him to be near enough to attack the king or First Pilgrim. How to do that and survive afterwards were two problems he'd have to study in calmer circumstances. It was hard to think straight with Anju nearby. Her strong personality was as intoxicating as her beauty.

"OK." She took her hand away. "You were going to show me more secret places."

"Only if they stay secret. Our secrets. You can't tell anyone, especially your uncle."

She frowned. "I'd never tell him anything. Or the First Pilgrim. Many days I want to run away from them."

"Where would you go?"

"Maybe I can join the Wilders."

"Risky. Your people behead them. They might do the same to you. You're safer here, at least for now." He stood and went to the opposite wall, reached up, and found the spot he was looking for. A panel slid open, revealing a dark corridor. He turned to her. "Your people have stolen our technology but not all our secrets. Are you coming?" He touched the receptacle on the right side of his head. Still there, he remembered its use more as magic than science.

"How does this work?" she said, touching the panel.

"The panel opens when an optical sensor tells it to." He noticed her raised eyebrow. "Many emit a laser beam that triggers the mechanism opening the door when it's interrupted. This one just senses when the light from the skylight dims as I cover it with my hand." He reached up again and the panel slid shut. Once more, and it slid open. "Come on."

"How do you know these things?" she said as he touched a panel on the inside wall, closing the panel again.

He put a finger to his lips. "Whispers. We will be going places where voices behind walls can be heard, and that can be dangerous. Your people are believers in magic. They will assume there are spirits in the walls. But the First Pilgrim and others know differently." He took her hand and led her along the corridor. Soft lights turned off behind them and came on in front. "To answer your question, I can't remember when I learned my way around the castle. Someone showed me long ago."

My mother? Should I tell her I'm the son of the Second Tribe's king? It was his father, of course, who constructed the secret doors and passageways, for both security and a playground maze for his offspring. He decided giving Anju more information wasn't a good idea. The less she knew, the less potential trouble for her. He wondered if he should even be showing her the secret places.

They walked for a long way. He saw her tense at every noise. One time he put his hand over her mouth to stifle a scream—he'd seen the vermin before she did. It was standing on its two hind feet, its red eyes gleaming at them. The fur was blotchy and it stank. He led her toward it, and it dashed off.

"What was that?"

"I don't remember the name. They can bite, but they're cowardly unless they're cornered. Many animals are like that." He smiled at her. "Even Humans."

Soon he opened another panel and they stepped into a large room with high walls and a domed ceiling. Frescoes were painted on the ceiling. They contained all sorts of creatures, including Humans.

"This is beautiful. Are all those creatures from the Second Tribe's legends?"

"I don't think so. Once someone told me they represent the sentient peoples from the known galaxy. This room is called the Creation Chapel. It celebrates the diversity of the Almighty Ra's Universe and Nut's unselfish creation of the planets Paradise and Eden for the Tribes. The frescoes were painted by one of our famous artists, a favorite of King Merson's predecessor. I heard he spent forty years doing it."

"It's beautiful," she said, taking a seat in the front row of seats. She pointed to the fresco behind the altar. "Who's the creature next to the Human?"

"He's called a Ranger. I have no idea why. They are very intelligent, so the legends say. Humans and Rangers made first contact long ago during dark times when both were fleeing their home planets."

"What were they fleeing from?"

He shrugged. "I have no idea. I don't know the whole story. Or can't remember. I heard it when I was a child. Maybe it's all myth, but I believe the Rangers are real. Some of their ships used to come here to Eden. They never went to Paradise?"

It was her turn to shrug. "I don't remember much about Paradise. I was a baby. I only know it became an ice world, and we had to take refuge here."

Kaushal looked away from her. *And we gave the First Tribe refuge, and yet they stole Eden from us.*

***

"Well done, boy," said King Breman. "Don't you agree, First Pilgrim?"

Gol Kovlyn inclined his head. His halo of hair framing his bald pate was white and unruly now. His eyes were always squinting through folds of fat. He sat back, hands folded over his paunch, and studied the boy, who sat politely and waited for the applause to end. He felt some primal stirrings. *Too bad this one is an entertainer. I could have some fun with him.*

The First Pilgrim surveyed the banquet hall. The king had become more corpulent than he was. The buffoon sat at the head of the long table with Kovlyn to his immediate right. *Had they spiked the punch?* The First Pilgrim had prohibited public displays of drunkenness long ago, but the king was swaying a bit. He had a long history of abusing liquor. *Or, had the royal chemists prepared a new designer drug for his highness to try?* That technology inherited from the Second Tribe helped to keep the masses under control, but the First Pilgrim didn't think it was appropriate for the ruling elites who needed little excuse for escapism.

Everyone had enjoyed the performance, especially Princess Anju. *What's going on there?* He wrote it off as simple infatuation for a good-looking fellow who was an entertaining musician. *How many women in the court have secret trysts with their slaves?* The aging king wasn't the image of a romantic lover, although there were drugs for that too.

His eyes returned to the boy. *He reminds me of someone.* Govlyn thought it shrewd of the lad that he had chosen officially sanctioned music to play and sing. *He will go far and be a favorite.* He might suggest to King Breman that it would be prudent to make him into a eunuch, though, like some other slaves. He smiled. It wouldn't please the king if he bedded Anju and discovered she was no longer a virgin. *You can't trust women these days.*

The musician played some more. After-dinner entertainment only ended when the king's chin fell to his chest, and he started to snore. *That is a common occurrence.* While courtiers helped the bloated sack to his quarters, the First Pilgrim approached the boy.

He held his instrument to his side so he could bow low.

"At ease, master musician. As the king said, you have done well. How did you come to the court?"

Kovlyn already knew. It was a test. People who lied to him often suffered for it. A particularly egregious lie would send the oaf to a public beheading. To lie to the First Pilgrim was to lie to the Almighty Ra or his daughter and son, Isis and Osiris.

The boy rattled off his history. His words contained more information than Kovlyn knew beforehand, so he was satisfied. A teetotaler, he was still lethargic from the meal.

"Your talent would be wasted as a common slave. You're now a master singer for King Breman's court. What say you to that, my lad?"

"If the king wishes," said the boy.

"The king is in no shape to wish for anything right now. I'll simply tell him he made you a master singer. He'll remember nothing, so he'll accept what I say." *And he would, even if he did remember. He knows he's replaceable.*

"I'm honored, First Pilgrim. It will be a pleasure to serve the court."

"Go grab your things and report to the head of security. He will show you your new quarters."

"Yes, sir."

The First Pilgrim watched Kaushal go. *Good lad, for a Second Tribe member.* He considered them only a bit more evolved than pond scum, but his one had a nice butt.

Chapter Five

The Voices

"We should learn more about this room," said Princess Anju.

Kaushal knew she had no idea where she was. He thought she might be dazzled by the scientific relics, but it was one place he had wanted to keep secret, so he was giving her a special treat.

"I have no idea what most of the things do," he said. "I was told commoners in the Second Tribe sometimes used these things, but they didn't understand how they work. All of this likely came in trade for our natural products and ores from our mines. After your people took over, those who understood a little were executed, so these things fell into disuse."

Again, he touched the side of his head in reflex. *What happened to all that information?* As a boy, people like old Benish weren't required. He would form the question in his head and the answer would be there. He missed that.

"Does any of it still work?"

"Some of it seems to. I play with things here, and sometimes they come to life."

"How do you know all these places?"

He shrugged. "Does it matter now? These things are meaningless to the First Tribe, and the Second Tribe has forgotten what they're here for. They're the decaying fossils of the civilization depicted in the frescoes." He grabbed a tablet and waved it at her. "This one, for example, comes to life sometimes. It looks a bit like the messenger tablets, but I suspect it was much more." Kaushal pressed buttons and icons and the screen lit up, but it only became a grayish white.

"Let me play with it." She pressed more buttons. The tablet started to speak. She dropped it. "Is it some kind of message?"

"Maybe. I don't recognize the language. It's not yours or mine." He meant the dialects of the First and Second Tribe. He listened. "It sounds a bit like what the merchants spoke. I didn't hear it often because I was just a boy."

"I recognize some words."

"I suppose we have words in common. Your and my languages are similar, for example. The merchants' language is probably older. Maybe our languages came from theirs."

There was a burst of static. Kaushal glanced at the tall windows that showed a darkening sky.

"Outside there's a storm," he said.

Lightning flashed. Another burst of static.

"It's like the voices are in the clouds," she said. "Can they be angels of the Almighty Ra?"

"Don't be naïve. There are no angels of the Almighty Ra. There isn't an Almighty Ra, at least not the one your people champion. Isis and Osiris are only drugged dreams of the Founder."

"That's blasphemy."

"Truth is blasphemy then. These are real Humans speaking, but they're likely voices from the grave. We called them recordings."

"OK, old wise one, why did the static occur with the lightning? Was that only coincidence?"

He laughed. "Probably not. The device is old. It's susceptible to static like our messenger tablets, only worse. That doesn't mean the voices come from live people."

***

The junk room became Princess Anju's favorite secret place. She would sit for hours working with devices while Kaushal would play and sing and secretly admire her beauty. One day he stopped playing and studied her.

"Don't they ever wonder where you are?" he said.

She glanced up from yet another tablet. "I can ask you the same question."

"I work at nights, so they let me sleep during the day. I'm technically sleeping. Fortunately, I need little rest. You don't have that excuse."

"Until I'm of age, I have the run of the castle. I hope the old lecher dies before I'm of age. I'd hate to have him put his hairy paws on me. I'd vomit."

He laughed. "I wouldn't blame you. Besides, he doesn't need another wife."

She cursed. "He's beheaded some of them for being infertile. Rumor has it he's the one who's infertile."

"In earlier days, that could be tested."

"Really? I wish I could prove it now. I wouldn't have to marry him."

Marrying him would be a tragedy, thought Kaushal. Voices interrupted his daydream about marrying the beautiful Anju.

"Look, people!"

He went to look over her shoulder.

"Merchants," he said.

On the screen, a Human male was talking. He was a tall man dressed in a uniform. A short beard and sunken cheeks gave him an ascetic appearance. *He looks more like royalty than either Breman or Kovlyn.*

The room he was in was bathed in a soft blue light. A row of people sat with their backs to him. They were monitoring large tablet screens pinned to walls. Some were adjusting controls.

"It's a spaceship," said Anju. "I remember. The First Pilgrim showed me something like this. I saw Eden from space."

"That's how you came here, of course," said Kaushal. "But look! Rangers!"

***

They studied the creatures from the frescoes. They were perched on special chairs and used some tentacles originating from around their mouths like hands.

"Is this a recording?" she said.

"I don't think so," he said. He pointed to one of the wall tablets seen on the device's screen. "Do you know what a map is?"

"Of course. I've seen maps of Paradise and Eden."

"Do you recognize what's on the screen?"

She looked closely. The entire tablet wasn't large, although it was mostly screen with a control bar on the bottom, so the screen in the background of the speaker in the strange uniform was even tinier. But she could see blue-green ocean and various islands.

"I'll bet that's Eden." She watched clouds flitting over islands in an archipelago. "There's the Big Island. See?"

"Yes. I can see Big Island with Dragon's Head in the north, Three Rivers Fjord in the south, Peace Bay to the west, and Hope Bay to the east. You can see the start of Founder's Channel by North Point too on that island that looks like a sheet flapping in the wind."

"I can maybe see the old volcano named Dragon's Mountain too. Is that a recording?"

"It could be. I don't know."

"Are they watching us?" Her eyes were big.

"I have no idea why they would. What's there to see? Maybe forests being cleared in the Northlands to make land for crops and some storms and clouds?"

"It would be creepy, that's all. They could zoom in, couldn't they? It would be like King Breman watching female slaves bathe using the spyglass."

"He does that?"

"I've heard he does. Maybe he even watches me."

Kaushal turned red with anger. "I should kill him!"

She laughed. "Would you like to watch me bathe?"

Fortunately his face was already red.

***

Seeing the merchants on the tablet motivated them to try to learn the language. Anju was good at it. She was also good at taking notes.

"It's clear our languages were derived from theirs," said Kaushal, days later.

"I'm more interested in what they're discussing. They are watching us. Not us personally, but Eden. They've put us into something they call a quarantine. I'm not sure what that means. In both our languages, a quarantine means separating the sick suffering a disease from those who don't suffer from it. But I don't think they're saying we're all sick."

"They're in orbit around our planet. I want to go there. I'd convince them to blow the First Pilgrim and King Breman into shredded pieces of bloody meat."

Anju frowned. "That's a bit violent. If they blow up Starlight Castle, they'd likely kill us both."

"Starlight Castle? You use our name?" She nodded. "I always wanted to go into space and visit the stars, but I often wondered why King Merson gave his castle that name. Even on darkest nights, it's hard to see stars from here. In the mountains, we could see many stars."

"You came from the mountains?"

"We were in hiding. Your soldiers found us. I prefer not to talk about it. They killed my mother."

"We have something in common. King Breman killed my father, and he killed your mother."

"Yet he's not the most dangerous."

"The First Pilgrim is." Kaushal nodded, making fists with his hands. "We can dream about punishing both of them for their transgressions and avenging my father and your mother."

She smiled.

Chapter Six

Discovery

During the next half of the Eden year, they explored the junk room's secrets and continued learning a bit of the strangers' language. It was frustrating. Sometimes Anju would be there, working alone; other times, Kaushal. When they were both there, they would have to bring each other up to date on what they'd learned.

"I wish we could communicate with them," said Anju one day.

Kaushal understood a bit of the merchants' language, but Anju could also speak it a little. It was an obvious wish for her to make.

"We're only intercepting their signals," he said. "Our communication systems are too primitive. We'd have to find a transmitter in this pile of junk, but I've seen nothing like that."

"Me neither," she said, "if you mean something that sends signals to them." She sighed. "It's frustrating, but what would we gain? They're only watching. None of them talk about helping us as far as I can determine."

"Maybe they would if they thought we were doing something about cleaning up Eden."

"You mean, attacking my uncle and the First Pilgrim and his people? You and I can't do that alone. We'd need help here on Eden."

He thought a bit. "Wilders. What do you know about them?"

"Rumors. Many courtiers say they're savages. But if they were, why would they stop some beheadings?"

"Good question. I've heard about them killing Royal Guards, and I'm all for that. When I've talked to cooking staff, my own people say they're heroes who are carrying on the fight. Even staff members who are First Tribe people shrug their shoulders and don't speak poorly of them."

"You talk to cooking staff?"

He smiled. "They still feed me tasty leftovers and rumors about the court and what's happening elsewhere in Eden. I give them songs. We both benefit. Sometimes groundskeepers and stable hands listen, and they have additional information. I want to know what's going on. We have to know if we're to have any success in overthrowing Breman and Kovlyn."

"You're clever. Do you know that, Kaushal?"

"I aim to please, my lady." He pointed at her lap. "You're bleeding."

She looked, jumped up, and dashed through the opening into the dark corridors.

***

Kaushal was puzzled. He didn't see Anju for a long time until he spotted her walking in the gardens surrounded by chaperones. *Was she sick?*

He worked in the junk room, but he couldn't stop wondering about her. When he figured it out, he understood her desperation. She had come of age. Chaperones had to be with her at all times until she married her uncle, King Breman.

He began to pace around the room in a rage. He had no hope Anju and he could ever be together, but the thought of her being with that bloated sack who was her scurrilous uncle made his ire peak. He had to stop that. *How can she marry the man who killed her father?*

One night a few days later, he was entertaining at a small dinner party the king had arranged for some rich princes and their consorts from the Northlands, the rich farming archipelago northwest of Big Island. Their ship had docked at the capital's largest wharf on Angel's Bay, its deck decorated for the night's festivities. Kaushal wasn't the only entertainment. A small orchestra also played dance music, slow enough so those drunk wouldn't fall and make a fool of themselves, and several comedians made the drunken revelers laugh.

Kaushal was enjoying himself when Anju made her appearance, surrounded by her chaperones. She bowed to King Breman, who kissed her hand. Kaushal wondered if she'd be in a hurry to wash that saliva off her hand. He would be. The drunken king had been drooling before Anju made her appearance. It was an indication the man was drugged or inebriated.

Anju and her entourage took their seats. That was Kaushal's cue.

He improvised, composing a sweet song about two lovers from old times whose families were feuding. The two ended their lives by poisoning themselves, crying until they died hugging each other. The audience loved it.

King Breman beckoned him. "A sweet but sorrowful song, lad," said the drunken lout in his slurred speech. He wiped away drool with the back of his hand. "I've never heard it. Is it a Second Tribe song?"

"No, sir. I just composed it. The party inspired me."

"Very good, very good. Are you hungry?"

"I can wait."

"I'll not hear of it. Go below to the galley kitchen. The chefs will fix you up. I'm so pleased I made you a master singer. I have a keen ear, you know."

As Kaushal passed by Anju, he smiled at her. Heading below deck, he smiled to himself. *Keen ear? The lout was about as musical as a belch.*

***

The next morning, two Royal Guards were waiting for him when he stepped from the shower. One threw him his clothing.

"You have to come with us," he said.

"Why? I entertained last night. I rest the morning after I work."

"You'll have some rest after your surgery," said the other with a laugh.

Surgery? Am I sick? No doctor's examined me except for the first time I returned to the castle.

The first soldier handed him a message tablet. It was a decree from the First Pilgrim. It read: *By order of the First Pilgrim, and in service to the Founder, the Almighty Ra, and his holy progeny, it is hereby decreed that the entertainer Kaushal shall be neutered so that he might take the special place of high-ranked master singer in King Breman's court and be able to serenade in the royal wedding between King Breman and Princess Anju.* An illegible signature followed, accompanied by religious symbols.

Kaushal looked at the soldiers. "If I refuse? Can I rejoin the kitchen staff?"

The first Guard shook his head. "Sorry, young man, you have no choice. First Pilgrim's orders."

Has Kovlyn detected their budding friendship? If so, he had chosen Anju's coming of age as the opportune moment to make Kaushal into a eunuch.

It took just seconds to decide he had no choice.

He handed the tablet back to the first Guard with his left hand and floored him with a right cross. The second reached for his gun, but Kaushal had stolen the first one's dagger and buried it in the second's heart before he could draw the weapon.

He contemplated the bloody scene for only a moment and then ran across the room to where he opened a panel. He disappeared into the bowels of the castle.

***

Kaushal knew he would have to flee to the mountains. Before that, though, he had two tasks. The first was visiting the junk room where he filled a bag with items he'd found useful. He also cleaned off the dagger there and stuck it in his belt. He headed for the area of the castle that housed the royal family.

He knew the first Guard would soon sound the alarm as soon as he became conscious, so he had to move fast. Hours spent playing games and exploring Starlight Castle now paid off. He could hear the snores even in the narrow passageway five meters away from the exit panel. He stepped out and stood at the side of the royal bed.

King Breman was still sleeping off his hangover.

Can I do this? I was protecting myself from the Guards. It's the First Pilgrim I want. This lout is only a threat to Anju!

"Did you know my father?" he said to the bloated sack, whispering in his ear. The man stirred. He repeated the question, only louder.

The man awoke with a start, staring at Kaushal with fright in his eyes.

"How-how did you come to be here, master singer? You're supposed to be having surgery."

"Aha, so you're in on it too, not just the First Pilgrim. Did you know my father, King Merson?"

The smell of fear, sweat, and poor toilet habits filled the room. Kaushal looked at the naked folds of fat—*the man can hardly walk*—and was filled with disgust. The king's beady eyes were bloodshot. *But does the man deserve to die?*

The fear seemed to increase. "What if I say yes?"

"How did he die?"

"He was beheaded with other members from the Second Tribe's court we apprehended."

Kaushal nodded. "Did you watch the beheadings?"

Sweat appeared on the king's upper lip. Nerves caused a fart and belch at the same time. He suffered a spasm; Kaushal smelled more urine.

"I had to."

Kaushal paced. *What should I do?*

The king's next action forced his decision. He jumped up and tackled Kaushal. Strong hands grasped at Kaushal's throat, pushing his thrashing body into the plush rug. Darkness was flooding into his mind when he found the dagger and thrust it into the massive chest in between two folds of fat surrounding the heart. The king rolled off Kaushal. Beady royal eyes glazed over.

Kaushal rested a bit, but he soon stood and vomited on top of the dead king. When the heaves stopped, he went back through the panel opening and closed it.

I'll have to seek my revenge with the First Pilgrim another day. At least Anju won't have to share this lout's bed!

Part Two

The Wilders Life

Two different groups comprised the opposition to the First Pilgrim, King Breman, and his successor. Mountain Folk were the smaller group, Wilders the larger. Both often attacked Royal Guards and public ceremonies involving palace favorites, interrupted executions, and stole from food and weapons depots, destroying what they left. They were disorganized at first but provided an easy scapegoat for the First Tribe's hegemony. One young leader organized them and provided motivation....

—Swims-in-Rapids, University of New Haven Professor of Sociology (translated from buzzspeak)

Chapter Seven

Mountain Folk

Kaushal's knowledge of secret corridors and spaces in Starlight Castle was so extensive that he had many choices for exiting. He chose an old entrance for provisions that soon led him into the narrow streets of a ghetto. People there were a mix of First Tribesmen down on their luck and Second Tribesmen who had returned to the city of Angels' Bay from hideouts in the mountains, but they were all so impoverished few paid much attention to origins.

He tore his pants and shirt and rubbed some dirt on his face before he left the castle. He didn't know the winding streets that well, but he soon found a pub. That time of morning the man at the bar was alone.

"No drinks, boy, unless you have coin," he said.

Kaushal offered one crown. He had a small stash from tips tossed to him as a performer.

The owner took the coin, bit into it to test its validity, and returned four of smaller denomination.

"What will you have, son?" he said with a smile.

Kaushal slid the four coins back at the man. "Information."

The man frowned. "What kind of information?"

"I need to flee to the mountains. Where do I go to find Mountain Folk?"

The man put an index finger to his lips, went to the door and looked both ways along the street, and then returned. "That kind of information will require another coin." Kaushal pushed another toward him. "You kill a Royal Guard or something?"

"Or something. I was an entertainer for King Breman."

"You'll be a Second Tribesman, I venture."

Am I in trouble? He speaks the First Tribe's dialect. "Does that matter?"

"Not to me. It'll matter to you if they catch you. You'll be praying for a simple beheading." He leaned forward across the bar. "Have a good memory, do you?"

"If I can remember hundreds of songs from both tribes, I can remember your directions, old man, if that's what you mean."

Directions for leaving the city were complicated, but they would take him to the highway over the mountains from Angels' Bay to Peace Harbor. Near the highest point, he would leave that highway. From there, directions became more complicated.

"Are there places to hide along the highway?" he said, figuring the highway might be well traveled and likely patrolled.

"Plenty of forest. If you're a smart lad, you can live off the land. There'll be wild nuts and berries and fish and game."

"I'll thank you then, good sir, and be off."

"I wish you luck, lad. You might be better off here in the ghetto, you know. Some First Tribe country folk might turn you in if they hear you're wanted by Guards. Mountain Folk won't—they don't care about First or Second Tribes— but you have to find them. Both choices are dangerous."

"I'll take my chances with Mountain Folk. You wouldn't be one who would turn me in, would you? You took my money."

46

He leaned forward again. "Let me tell you a secret: I'm Second Tribe too, and I served in King Merson's personal security force. I managed to escape the purge. I harbor no love for any of that bunch who killed him."

Was it a ploy to make him admit what he'd done? Kaushal hated to be so paranoid, but his life was at stake. "Maybe things will change," was all he said.

He stopped at the pub's entrance and scanned the street as the pub owner had done. He then headed off on his trek.

***

That afternoon a squad of soldiers went by the pub. The owner went outside to watch as the squad went to the intersection where twenty of them split off two by two, working their way towards him, pounding on doors, and breaking in if there was no answer. Those who answered their doors were pushed inside. The pub's owner figured they were searching houses.

Five remaining soldiers started tacking wanted posters onto power poles, again working toward the pub. There was a pole right outside the pub's entrance, so the owner read the poster.

WANTED FOR REGICIDE! ran across the top of the poster. The pub owner read on: *Court entertainer and Second Tribesman Kaushal is wanted for regicide and other assorted crimes. All citizens of Eden are required to provide any available information about his whereabouts on pain of death. A reward of ten thousand crowns is offered for any information leading to his arrest. By order of the First Pilgrim.*

The pub's owner struggled to keep from smiling because the soldier who had posted the circular was watching him. *Ha! I should have given that lad money and drinks for a job well done! And they're only offering ten thousand crowns?*

"Know anything about this fellow Kaushal, Pilgrim?" said the soldier.

"No sir," said the pub's owner. "I'd collect the reward if I did. How'd he manage to do this evil deed?"

The soldier shrugged. "I've only heard rumors. The Royal Guards say he's the Devil's henchman and can materialize and disappear from thin air. I've also heard said they're not sure he's who did the king in, but this entertainer can't be found. They're even questioning a princess."

"Maybe a little love affair in the court?" said the pub's owner with a wink.

The soldier looked around and then back at the pub's owner. "Keep those thoughts to yourself, old man. People are going to lose their heads for this one. And anyone helping this villain will be praying for that as the easy way out."

"Thank you for the advice. Can I offer you a drink?"

"Some other time. I'm on duty, can't you see?"

"Drop by later then."

When the pub is full, and I have enough regulars who'll want to beat the crap out of you.

***

Kaushal took two days to reach the point where he had to leave the highway. Squads of soldiers patrolled the highway, so he often had to hide. They would pour from huge troop carriers and search areas around the highway. They were trying to find someone. He figured that someone would be him.

But the old man had been right: Kaushal could live off the land, and there was plenty of water because the highway followed curves in the Angels' River. At one point the river forked, though, and he had to dash across the bridge over the North Fork because the highway followed the South. If a squad had come along the highway at that moment, he would have been exposed.

On the bridge's other side, the forest thinned a little, but there was still adequate cover even as the highway climbed into the hills. At one point, he stopped to admire the view of Angels' Bay and the capital with the same name he had left; it was toward the northeast, and the city of Long Beach at the entrance to Hope Bay toward the east. The view of most of that bay and the eastern islands of the archipelago was blocked by tall mountains, but none as tall as Dragon's Mountain, the extinct volcano to the north always topped with snow.

After he left the main highway, patrols diminished in number. He saw other troubling signs, though—burned-out hovels, crops in the fields around them withering in the sun; vehicles stripped and burned; a skeleton still hanging from a noose in a tree; a crashed helicopter; and a lack of animals.

Humans are the most savage of all animals. Hadn't he committed savagery himself? It wasn't any consolation that the king would have killed him. Even half asleep, the despot had the strength of three men. Odors of the man's alcoholic breath and hedonistic night were still fresh in Kaushal's memory.

The third night he was starting to wonder where he was going. The pub's owner had spoken of a three-tiered waterfall he'd have to climb. On top, he was to follow the creek's ravine. But it was the dry season. *Will that small creek still be flowing, on its way to join Angels' River?*

He'd found some berries and caught a small animal he skinned and cooked. Its meat was strong and oily and needed salt, but he ate most of it, knowing he needed the protein. Salt would only make him thirsty. He'd have to find that waterfall for that reason too.

***

Kaushal awoke with a spear at this throat. A woman held the spear steady.

He studied her. She was older than he was. Close-cropped black hair framed a tanned but pretty face. She looked athletic; muscled arms held her long weapon steady. She was dressed in kilt and sandals with leather laces up her legs. She looked angry.

Proud breasts pointed at him as if they were accusing him of being her enemy. A necklace made from shells of sea creatures hung in her cleavage. Her midriff ended in a puckered naval followed by the colorful kilt held up by a leather belt. From it hung a pistol and sword.

He couldn't help staring at the rustic warrior.

"Give me one reason why I shouldn't kill you," she said.

"I killed King Breman."

She laughed and the sharp blade of the spear nicked his throat. "A true reason, pretty boy, not a fictional tale. We don't like liars from Angels' Bay around here."

"I can understand that. But I'm not lying. Have you noticed the increased frequency of patrols?" She nodded. "They're after me. I was an entertainer in the king's court. They were going to turn me into a eunuch."

She stepped back but still held the spear ready. He noted archers in the shadows who lowered their bows only a bit.

"An entertainer? No wonder you're stupid enough to eat a drax. Anything tastes better."

He propped up on his elbows. "I eat what I can catch. I don't have much choice."

She cocked her head and thought a moment. "So how did you entertain the king and all his court?"

"I sang."

"Sing me a song then."

He frowned. "I don't have my roki. I had to leave it behind."

"Sing me a song without it. True master singers don't need accompaniment."

He nodded and began to sing a Second Tribe song, one he would never dare sing in King Breman's court.

"Stop!" He did so and noticed her eyes were moist. "My mother used to sing me that song. How did you know?"

"Coincidence. It's a nice and easily sung Second Tribe song I can sing *a capella*. My mother sang it to me too."

"I don't know what *a capella* means." She looked back at her companions. Some of them nodded. "You'll come with us. What's your name?"

"Kaushal, son of Mela, King Merson's first wife."

The others gasped and they all came forward and kneeled. It wasn't how people kneeled in the court of King Breman, though. Kaushal remembered it well from King Merson's court—a drop to one knee with only a slight bowing of the head, a simple sign of respect for the Second Tribe's king, not an obsequious display from sycophants.

"Please, those times are past. Right now I'm only an entertainer running for his life." He laughed. "And so dumb I eat drax."

The woman stood and offered him a hand. "My name is Kifi. It is foretold that a royal warrior will come to lead us and return Eden to its glory days. You must be him."

"I doubt it. I let you capture me. Some warrior."

Kifi smiled. "You will learn." She winked and blew a kiss at him. "I can teach you many things." The others laughed. "Come. We have a ways to go, and the day isn't getting any longer."

Chapter Eight

Journey to the Mountain Folk's Village

Kaushal followed Kifi, and the rest followed behind, often in single file. The sway of the woman's hips in front of him was mesmerizing. He figured she was about ten years older, the woman Anju would become now that she had come of age. He felt a lusty attraction for Kifi nonetheless.

He wondered what her role was among Mountain Folk. She had to be some sort of leader. Those following her were five men and three women, all young and healthy. *Were they on patrol? Had they committed the mayhem he had seen after turning off the main highway?*

The three-tiered falls had been reduced to a trickle. He might have found it, but it was certainly easier following Kifi. They followed the ravine until they came to a spot where water poured from a small opening in a cliff.

"We'll rest here," she said.

After everyone quenched their thirst, Kaushal took a lotus position on a flat rock and found some pieces of drax he had brought with him. Kifi plopped down beside him.

"Toss that into the bushes, you fool. It's only fit to be food for bugs and microbes. Here, try this."

She handed him dried meat. He tried it and found it full of flavor.

He smiled at her. "I probably should learn what animal this comes from."

"It's called a jonki. We herd them. Domesticated beasts. When we fled into the hills, we brought them with us. You'll like the steaks and smoked bacon even better."

"Are you farmers?"

"Warriors and farmers. We rotate jobs. That way everyone knows everything and can do what's necessary to survive. We don't have an easy life, but it's better than living in the ghettos of Angels' Bay. We live off the land and move from time to time. Farmers. Nomads. All old words."

"Words are my trade. I tell stories with my songs."

"Some of us do that too. But those who do must still contribute. Life isn't easy in the mountains. The good land is in the foothills and plains, especially the flood plains of Angels' River. But we survive."

"You're older than I am. You probably remember the purge better. I was only a young boy when they killed my mother and kidnapped me."

"I was old enough to serve as entertainment for the First Tribe's soldiers. The last one was still brutalizing me when I slit his throat and fled."

"Those are bad memories. I'm sorry I asked."

"I'm glad you did. I need to keep those memories alive. My desire for revenge feeds off them." She looked at the blue sky. "Some days it's the only reason I have for getting up."

***

After eating and resting, some of the group held vines aside that hid a cave in the cliff wall. The pub's owner had called it a passageway. Kaushal knew he never would have found it. They followed the cave until they emerged on a ledge overlooking a small valley surrounded by steep lava walls.

"Dragon's Mountain isn't the only extinct volcano," said Kifi. "This whole mountain chain and Big Island originated during Eden's volcanic past."

The scene was one of pastoral beauty. Lush grasslands were interrupted by copses of trees lining creeks and rivers. Kaushal saw herds of animals tended by children. A cluster of hovels emitted lazy wisps of smoke that wafted in the breeze as if to beckon him home. It was another world compared to over-populated Angels' Bay.

"Wouldn't you be trapped here if the First Tribe sealed off the cave?" he said.

She cocked her head and thought a moment. "Two comments: Here there isn't any First Tribe or Second Tribe, only Mountain Folk. We accept everyone and expect everyone to contribute. And there are many ways in and out. This one isn't even the easiest. We have to go there." She pointed down a steep lava slope. The cliff, pocked in places where ancient magma bubbles had burst, was mostly covered with volcanic rubble.

"I'm not capable of doing that," he said. "Is there another way?"

Others in the group laughed.

"There are many ways. I said we have to go there. I didn't say how. There's a trail with switchbacks along the rim that's not too steep a route, for example. Follow me, and watch your footing. Step where I do, or you'll be falling down the mountain to your death."

It took some time, but once below they followed a river he had seen from above meandering toward the village. The valley soil was rich. Kaushal even saw orchards with fruit trees. The fruit looked like it was still ripening.

"You might be nomads, but you've been here awhile," he said as the troop entered the village.

"The orchards can fend for themselves. We always move on after a harvest so we can burn stubble left over from crops. That returns nutrients to the soil. We take the livestock with us."

"And where do you go?"

"Along the mountain chain there are refuges, hidden valleys like this one."

"Aren't you worried about flyovers?"

"Only the First Tribe's inter-island hoppers fly high enough to pass over these peaks. Local flights like military transports fly too low. The First Tribe's soldiers don't like the mountains."

"Because of the snow?"

"No. We don't go that high." She smiled. "They don't like the mountains because they become our targets. We own the mountains, so they're scared of their own shadows."

"Why don't they kill all of you?"

"We own the mountains," she said again. "The more they send, the more who die."

"We never heard about that in Angels' Bay," he said.

"Why would they tell you? They want to make it look like they're in control. They control less than half of Big Island, and in the Southlands they have no control at all."

"Where Wilders are."

"That's what the First Tribe calls them. They were Mountain Folk like us. In fact, some attacks attributed to Wilders are only us making life difficult in Angels' Bay." She stopped in front of a hut a bit bigger than the others. "We're here. Let's go inside."

"Am I going to meet your leader?" said Kaushal as Kifi pulled aside a canvas serving as a curtained door blocking the entrance.

"We don't have leaders like the First Tribe or Second Tribe's kings. Tristan is more like our First Pilgrim."

Kaushal hesitated. "I'm not armed."

"Silly, he's like the First Pilgrim only because he's a spiritual leader as well as a warrior. Come on. He's probably in his workshop. He loves to tinker. Maybe too much."

***

"So, this is the master singer," said the man looking up from his workbench.

He was examining something like what Anju and Kaushal had found inside broken electronic tablets. Every so often he would touch a small pistol to the board, and a little curl of smoke would rise. They waited. He finally swung around on his stool and stood.

He was about Kaushal's size. His hair was in disarray. Bronzed and muscular, he only wore a plain loincloth. His eyes were green and seemed full of mischief. They had epicanthic folds Kaushal had seen in some First Tribesmen.

The smile looked genuine. He offered his hand. Kaushal went forward to grasp it in greeting. Tristan shook his head.

"The bag," he said.

"It's mine."

"Not any more. Mountain Folk don't own property, lad. We can't afford to do that. Being attached to things keeps you from following the Way."

"The Way?"

"I'll explain later," said Kifi. "Hand him the bag. He knows how to use what you brought, or he wouldn't ask."

Kaushal shrugged and handed the bag to Tristan who dumped its contents on another workbench. He rummaged around a bit in the pile.

"Some good items here. Even the junk can have its uses. We always need spare parts. Where did you obtain all this?" Kaushal explained. "In other words, you stole it. Good fellow. We need it more than the First Tribe. Besides, I'm not sure they'd know what to do with it." He picked up a tablet, thought a moment, eyed Kifi, and stared at Kaushal. "Have you communicated with them?"

"Who? People on the ship?"

"Ah, you've seen them, but not communicated. Possibly the transmitters are damaged or the batteries low. Pity. Kifi, please leave now. This young person and I need to have a little talk."

Kifi frowned. "I want to stay. And I need to show him around."

"There'll be time for that. Don't worry, I won't damage him."

She blushed. "You have impure thoughts, Tristan."

"Possibly. But Humans have lusted after one another for ages. Fortunately, that's more common between those of opposite sexes. If you didn't procreate, your species would have disappeared in the galactic nebulas of time, but, of course, not everyone needs to participate in that." He smiled at the now fading blush. "Leave us now. I'll bring him to you soon enough."

"You talk strange," said Kaushal, finding a stool and sitting. "And wasn't that a harsh way to treat Kifi? She deserved to hear what we have to say."

"She's a beautiful woman who needs to control her emotions sometimes. And she's filled with hatred for the First Tribe. We all need to work on that, but of course it's understandable people feel that way. Such emotions get in the way of logic and reason, though."

"I feel the same way," said Kaushal. Tristan nodded and smiled. "What do you need to talk to me about?"

"What you saw. You have to promise to keep it to yourself. Kifi has already heard too much—one reason she wanted to stay. Perhaps the time will come when it doesn't matter, but right now these people shouldn't know there are those who can help them."

"People on the ship?"

"Unfortunately you know it's a ship. Do you know where it is?"

"It's not only a video recording then. They're up there...in orbit?"

Tristan nodded. "By their laws, they cannot interfere." He put his hands on his hips and studied Kaushal. "You look like him a bit."

"Who?"

"King Merson. I knew him well."

"You knew my father?"

"Long ago. Why would you go to live in King Breman's court if you knew your past?"

"For revenge."

"Ah yes, another Human with wild emotions. Did you murder King Breman?"

"It was more an accident, but the court and the First Pilgrim won't see it that way. I had to leave Anju behind."

"The princess who was promised to the murdered king? Interesting. Who will she marry now?"

"Me, hopefully."

"Not likely, lad. She probably hates you now."

"Not likely, Tristan." Kaushal had mimicked the man's clipped speech; he smiled. "She hated the king. He killed her father."

"Hmm, yes. I see. She's why you have no interest in Kifi."

"Anju helped me study all these devices. She's good at figuring them out."

"I can see some possibilities there. Tomorrow we will head for the Southlands."

"What? I just arrived."

"Kifi will go too. Tonight we party."

"A party? For me?"

"Of course not, you mindless drax." Tristan guided him toward the hovel's entrance. "Don't be filled with self-importance. It's the start of the harvest. We have two per year here. Partying puts everyone in the mood to work extra hard."

"But won't they need us for the harvest?"

"They need us more in the Southlands."

Chapter Nine

Journey to Peace Harbor

Tristan faced them. He was now dressed in something like a calf-length skirt, a colorful kilt—they all were. There were no scars, so Kaushal figured the Mountain Folk's leader had never been in battle, although a long knife hung in a scabbard at his waist and a rifle was in a holster on his back. Ammo for the gun was contained in a soft leather belt running from his right shoulder to left hip and across his back. His commanding presence left no doubt who was in charge of the expedition, yet he also projected an aura of humility. He was a warrior-priest.

"Followers of the Way can always choose," he said to them. "If anyone has second thoughts, be assured this mission will be dangerous. We might all perish. Those in doubt should stay and help with the harvest. Our leaving will create a personnel shortage. Do you understand your choices?"

They all nodded. Tristan had halted the festivities the night before to ask for four volunteers to join Kifi, Kaushal, and him. Many had volunteered. Tristan chose and the party continued.

Maybe he suspected some volunteers were only inebriated? thought Kaushal.

After the party, Kifi and others had explained some teachings of the Way. Kaushal was doubtful. While the teachings sounded more practical and logical than teachings of the First Pilgrims and the Founder, he wasn't able to discern much difference. There was no Almighty Ra, but if you took the intent of the Founder's message to heart and not the variations created by many religious leaders who had followed later, the moral code wasn't all that different. But he didn't understand the idea of enlightenment.

"Few attain it," Kifi had said.

"What about Tristan?"

"He's never said. And no one asks."

Tristan brought Kaushal back to the present.

"Fine. Let's move out. Scouts in front."

Kifi left Kaushal and took the lead. Tristan dropped back to the middle of the column to walk behind Kaushal.

They left the valley by a different route from when Kaushal had entered. He looked back a few times at the beautiful vista. *I hope I'll be able to return.*

***

They headed west. After two days of treacherous trails, they rounded a bend and stopped to enjoy another inspiring view below.

"Peace Bay, Peace Harbor, and the town by the same name," said Tristan, knowing Kaushal had never been there.

"Are we going into town?"

"Not quite. Maybe some other time you can explore this side of Big Island."

"Except for escaping to the mountains when the First Tribe defeated us," said Kaushal, "I've been a city boy. My previous life was entertaining in King Breman's court for the most part."

"You don't remember King Merson's court?"

"I remembered secret passages and hidden places in his castle. They were my playground as a boy. That came in handy."

61

Tristan nodded. "That's past. Let's focus on the future. We have another three day trek ahead of us. Our destination isn't as close as it looks. We might as well begin it."

As they walked, Tristan explained that early on they had thought of stealing vehicles from the Royal Guards or merchants, but the idea had floundered in the sea of good intentions and dashed hopes because they realized they would have to keep stealing fuel too, adding more risk to an already precarious existence. So they walked.

Tristan was wrong, though. They arrived in two days, the trek ending by climbing a promontory a few kilometers southwest of the town of Peace Harbor. Kaushal saw a small village below with some fishing boats.

"Is that our destination?" he said.

"If it's safe," said Kifi. "You have a bounty on your head now. You're a liability in a sense, but you're worth it. Don't let it go to your head, though."

He smiled. Her brusque words contained a bit of sweetness, although she didn't smile. The long hike had tired everyone except Tristan, who looked as fresh as ever. *Maybe there's something to this Way,* he thought. He had seen their leader in meditation many times, a frozen statue staring at the horizon.

"We'll enter right after dark." Tristan lowered his binoculars and smiled at Kifi. "Rolf can offer sanctuary in his basement like before."

"That lewd lout?" said Kifi. "We should go straight to the ship. He's a smelly one, he is."

"The boat can't leave before dawn due to the dark and fog this time of year," said Tristan. "Don't worry, my dear. Kaushal and I will protect you from Rolf."

"That won't stop him from drooling all over Ezan and me."

Ezan, the other woman in the party, was younger than Kifi. She lowered her binoculars too. She pulled a knife and waved it at them.

"Don't worry. I'll threaten to make him a eunuch. He'll behave or lose the family jewels, not that they're much good for anything anymore."

"He can get you all drunk," said Tristan, "and you would be helpless. That's not a good idea even without Rolf, considering soldiers in the local garrison have been known to frequent his tavern. I recommend we lay off alcohol until we arrive where we want to go." He pointed to his left where there was forest. "We'll take the long way through the woods and rest at their edge until nightfall. Be as quiet as possible. I spotted soldiers on patrol in some streets."

"I saw some breaking down a door to a house." Ezan smiled at Kaushal. "They're not dumb. They know where you're going. It's the logical next step, you see. I hope we're not walking into a trap."

"And that's why we must be careful. We must deliver Kaushal."

"So, am I a package now?" said Kaushal.

"No, you're a valuable asset for our cause because people will follow you," said Tristan. "Right now you're our best bet for real change. But, as Kifi said, don't let it go to your head."

"I won't, don't worry. I don't feel special. I'm still just an entertainer."

"You're more than that, lad. And don't be tempted to sing your songs at Rolf's pub. The First Pilgrim has spies everywhere."

Kifi hooked her arm into his. "You can sing to me when we arrive in the Southlands. I like your voice even if Tristan doesn't."

Tristan frowned at her. But they gathered their weapons and supplies and moved out.

***

Some servers from Rolf's pub, The Green Dragon, brought them a meager, cold repast to them in the dark basement where they were hiding. Rolf had bid farewell hours ago and headed upstairs to attend to his customers.

Kaushal had found Kifi's lewd lout to be a friendly, soft-spoken giant with biceps as big around as Kaushal's thighs. He took Kaushal by the shoulders and stared into his eyes.

"I see our old king," he said. "I'll follow you, lad. You're from good stock. You'll galvanize the people to overthrow the First Tribe's despots."

Kaushal was becoming embarrassed with the attention. He also didn't want to disappoint anyone, but he knew he had no special fighting skills. He had been lucky with King Breman, and he'd been no warrior. *Can I learn? Why bother? I don't want to be king!*

"Why green dragon? I know the mountain is called Dragon's, but what is a dragon and why is this one green?" Kaushal later asked after they had supper. He used some coarse black bread to absorb the watery stew's remains.

"It's a creature that often appears in Earth's folklore," said Tristan.

"Is that our home world? And how do you know this?"

Tristan paused to consider his questions. Kaushal noticed he hadn't eaten a thing.

"The answer to your first question is maybe, but I don't have all the facts. For the second question, does it matter? You can either believe what I say or believe it's a lie. I don't care either way." A server came downstairs and whispered in his ear. "Whether you're all through or not, we need to clear the tables and stack them as they were originally so it looks like they're here in storage. And then we must hide."

"Where?" said Kaushal.

Tristan pointed to several tall storage closets lining the walls. "This kind woman will lock us in, and Rolf will insist we're only gardening tools. He has a nice garden in back, by the way."

They hid in the closets and the serving lady went back upstairs with the utensils and dishes. In a few minutes, they heard Rolf's voice, sounding distant and muted for such a large man.

"I must protest," he said after Kaushal heard many heavy boots come down the stairs. "I'm a loyal citizen of King Breman's realm. Why are you searching my establishment?"

"We have orders to search everywhere," said one soldier in a gravelly voice. "What's in there?"

"Nothing but gardening tools," Rolf said.

"Why are the bins locked?" said another soldier.

"Good tools are hard to come by. My help steals from me all the time. They're good people, but they're poor. You know. The poor often steal. What they can't use, they sell. That's just the way it is."

"Second Tribe scoundrels, I'd say," said the first soldier. "If they're only tool storage units, you won't mind if Rispok runs his sword through them."

Kaushal heard heavy boots approaching his bin. He squeezed into a back corner, trying to make himself small. The blade still nicked him in the side, but he swallowed his scream of pain.

"Enough," said the first soldier. "We're wasting our time here. Kill that drax!"

Was he going to kill Rolf? Kaushal was ready to jump from the storage bin and do battle but remembered he was locked inside just in time. He heard a chase followed by a familiar squeal. *A real drax in the basement had gone to join his ancestors.* He smiled.

"I suggest you clean up that mess," said the soldier.

Kaushal heard them ascending the stairs.

***

"That was close," Kifi said as she dressed Kaushal's small but bloody wound. "They had rifles and could have riddled all the bins."

"They're only the First Pilgrim's soldiers because they're too stupid to be anything else," said Rolf, inspecting her handiwork. He put the cork in the liquor bottle—Kifi had cleansed the wound with the fiery liquid. "They want you, lad. You'd best leave the village as fast as you can. Your life is in danger."

"We'll be going soon," said Tristan. "It's almost dawn."

"Hard to tell in this basement," said Kaushal.

"For you," said Kifi. "The gloom and dampness here made the soldiers want to leave as soon as possible, not to mention the stench."

"Excuse me?" said Rolf. "Some of that stench comes from you folks."

Kaushal stifled a laugh. Old Rolf stank of sweat and liquor.

"Not I," said Tristan, "but let's change the topic. Did you arrange everything with your brother?"

"He doesn't know if he can find enough crewmembers on this short notice," said Rolf. "Are any of you sailors?" said Tristan, looking at his group.

Ezan and one of the men raised their hands. "We're from Peace Harbor originally," Ezan said. "It's been a while. And Kifi is familiar with boats—she dives."

Ezan was somewhere between the ages of Anju and Kifi and just as pretty. If she knew how to sail, that raised her stature in Kaushal's eyes. He loved to sail but knew little about the necessary skills, and he knew nothing about diving.

Kifi caught him studying Ezan and punched him in the shoulder, giving him a warning look. *Is she jealous? Or, is she protecting the younger woman?*

"You can brush up on your skills as we go," said Tristan. He examined Kaushal's bandage. "Is that wound going to cause you problems?"

"Don't worry about me," said Kaushal. "It's just a scratch. A bit painful, but it looked worse than it was. Shall we get ready?"

"Let's ask Rolf to go see if the way is clear." He smiled at the heavyset, bearded man. "Would you be so kind, my friend?"

"Let's wait a bit. We're packing some provisions for you."

"We can't carry much," said Kifi.

"My dear, I wouldn't think of it. Besides, I can't afford it. They're only the basics. Nutritious but compact." They waited until the serving lady appeared at the head of the stairs and nodded to Rolf. "OK. Now you can pack up, and I'll check the street."

Kifi fell back as they were leaving and planted a kiss on Rolf's cheek. "You might not see me again," she said, "so that's to keep my memory alive."

"Kifi, there's no way I'd forget my best friend's daughter. Have a safe voyage. I'll see you soon enough, don't worry."

"I didn't know you two were friends," Kaushal said to her in a whisper as they paused in a dark alley waiting for a patrol to pass.

She put her finger to her lips and then showed him crossed fingers. "My father and Rolf were like this. He's still a lewd lout."

"Let's move out," said Tristan.

Chapter Ten

En route to the Southlands

They were onboard in the hold of the ship before Kaushal renewed the conversation with Kifi.

"Where's your father then?"

"Dead. He was killed by a patrol not far from where we captured you."

"I'm sorry."

"For what?" Kifi cocked her head and looked at the deck above her head. "You didn't kill him. You've had your own tragedies."

"Don't remind me. The desire for revenge still eats at my insides."

"You have to get beyond that. You have responsibilities now."

He considered her advice. Wasn't she the person accused by Tristan of having revengeful emotions? "Because Tristan says so?"

"Because Eden needs you. It isn't about you anymore, Kaushal. Please realize that. Or about me. I have to be careful to control and focus my hate. For you, it's essential."

He sighed. "Maybe I don't want that responsibility. My life was simpler in the court."

"Despots always foment complacency and ignorance. They are tools for manipulating the suffering masses. You have no idea about how organized we are, but we need an iconic leader to serve as glue."

He smiled. "So I'm supposed to be an iconic leader? I almost was killed hiding in a tool bin. Some leader!"

She thought a moment. "That's an interesting thought. Tristan! We might have a spy!"

Tristan glanced up from a tablet. "Say again?"

"Why did the soldier choose Kaushal's tool bin? What told him to choose that one? I don't believe in coincidences."

"Hmm. Good point. We were all in bins. There was no way for him to know." Tristan stood. "And I heard nothing to direct attention to Kaushal's bin. A related question: why did they come to Rolf's pub first? There are five taverns in the village." He thought a bit. "Come here, Kaushal."

Tristan began examining him. After finishing the top, he said, "Take off your kilt."

Kaushal glanced at Ezan and Kifi, and the two women smiled and then giggled. The long, calf-length kilt often had nothing underneath, especially at lower altitudes with the heat and humidity. He had followed Mountain Folk custom.

"There!" said Tristan, pointing to a small scar on Kaushal's hip. "Kifi, hand me your dagger. I'll need some of Rolf's spirits too."

Kaushal couldn't remember being naked in front of a woman. He thought of Anju, looked at the low ceiling, and didn't worry too much about Ezan and Kifi.

They had brought a flask of liquor for medicinal purposes. Tristan swabbed the spot on Kaushal's hip. With the dagger, he dug into flesh and soon showed them a small disk about the size of a small button.

"These can be easily implanted," said Tristan. "You have no recollection?"

"I don't even know what it is," he said.

"It's called a tag. It emits a weak electronic signal pursuers can follow with the right equipment. When you became an entertainer for the court, did you undergo a medical exam?"

"No, I had one when I arrived at the castle as a slave. The doctor said I was a fine physical specimen, but he gave me some injections—one in that place, I think."

"Yes, you are built like a jonki breeding stallion." The two women tittered and the men smiled. "But that one injection probably allowed him to place this disk. And now they might be hoping you lead them to the main Wilders force. The First Pilgrim and his lackeys are devious. They can capture you and destroy that force at the same time."

"That's where we're going, isn't it?"

Tristan examined the disk and smiled. "Yes, but thanks to Kifi, now I'm considering using their own tool. We will use this disk to convince whoever is following you to walk into a Wilders' trap. But, for now, the damage is done, and it's my responsibility."

"Maybe I'm the spy," said Kaushal. "Can I put my kilt back on?"

"Sure. But you need a bandage. Kifi, we need your good hands again."

He watched Kifi clean the small wound and bandage it. Nodding his approval, Kaushal redressed. "Why is it your responsibility?"

"You had no idea you were tagged," said Tristan, "but I knew it's common practice in the court. It was in Merson's court too. Both nobles and servants are tagged. It's a simple bit of Second Tribe technology that still exists."

"So, let's hear about your plan for a trap," said Kifi, flashing an evil smile.

***

The archipelago Eden natives called the Southlands had many more islands than the one containing Big Island and the capital, Angels' Bay. It took them seven days of sailing, but they didn't dock at their intended destination.

From there, Tristan sent for representatives from the fierce southern tribes the rest of Eden knew as Wilders. These were Mountain Folk who had migrated and become fierce warriors and bold sailors.

"I like your plan," said an old man.

Kaushal had been studying these Wilders. There were three of them, big fellows with rippling muscles and torsos filled with tattoos. They all shaved their heads but wore large hats woven from some kind of grassy strands and decorated with colorful cloth bands. Their kilts weren't one color either.

The old man's face was lined and his cheeks sunken. He still looked strong. The other two were younger. They were named Petro, Samos, and Kindri.

Samos and Kindri could pass for Mountain Folk except for their garb, validating Kifi's tale that they were Mountain Folk who migrated from the mountains. They were more impetuous while Petro took his time pondering the nuances of a situation. Kaushal liked all of them. Like Mountain Folk, they were more optimistic and energetic than most people he had known in Angels' Bay. Even nobles there had only gone through the motions because of the oppressive weight of the First Pilgrim's theocracy.

Petro studied Kaushal for a moment. "Are you willing to be bait? They will be intent on killing us, but you have to expect torture until you ask for mercy with a beheading if they catch you. You look like your father but have your mother's disposition, by the way."

"You knew my mother and father?"

"I was a general in your father's Royal Guard, one of King Merson's elite soldiers. I saw many companions slaughtered. Many who were caught were later beheaded. We make attempts to stop some beheadings even now, but the

First Pilgrim and his men have learned to be devious. Our distance from the capital hinders our efforts too."

"After our journey, I can imagine what it takes to mount an attack on Angels' Bay."

"Enough chitchat," said Tristan. "Petro's question still stands, Kaushal. We want to use you to bait the trap."

"I'm up for it. I don't plan to be captured. I'll kill myself first."

"We don't want that. As far as we know, you're the only remaining person who can be Eden's legitimate king."

"That's silly. If we ever rid Eden of the First Tribe's despots, why do we need a king?"

"To do that, we need a king to rally the people," said Petro. "No one cares if you abdicate after that, as far as I'm concerned."

"There would be a lot of instability when the power vacuum is created," said Tristan. "We might want Kaushal to continue being king for a while."

Petro shrugged. "Maybe. We're loading the cart before we know the jonki can pull it. Let's set this trap first. How many First Tribesmen can we expect?"

***

"Those tactical discussions were boring," said Kaushal.

They were back on the boat now. Petro and the other two had sailed three days ago to organize forces needed to surround the First Pilgrim's men. Kaushal now carried the little disk in a little bag at his waist.

"But necessary," said Kifi, scanning the horizon.

They could now see their original destination, the Wilders' main island stronghold. They changed its location from time to time, but it would have been a disaster if the First Pilgrim's men had caught them unawares.

"Petro is a clever fellow," said Kaushal.

"Like the rest of us, he's a survivor. Unlike you, he hasn't tasted revenge yet."

"What's his story?"

"His mother and sister were raped and beheaded as punishment for not telling the First Pilgrim's Guards where Petro was. Of course, they had no idea, so they couldn't tell. Their heads, along with others, hung in the town square for weeks until larva ate their brains."

Kaushal shuddered. "That must have been at the same time we were escaping to the mountains," he said. "He doesn't seem bitter."

"He has learned the sweetest revenge can be found in well laid plans to annoy and frustrate the First Pilgrim's men. He has become an expert at it. The enemy has no idea who or where he is."

"It wouldn't be good to lose him then," said Kaushal.

"We all will die sometime," said Kifi with a shrug.

"I hope we die battling these bastards instead of from old age."

"That is the Wilders' attitude, the same attitude of Mountain Folk," she said. "But try to stay healthy for a time yet. You heard the discussion. You're needed for further plans."

"Yes, that iconic leader role again." He put a hand on her shoulder. "After this trap business is over, I want you to teach me to be a warrior. I have many things to learn."

"You've already learned the most important thing."

"Oh, what's that?"

"Enough humility to know you have many things to learn," she said with a laugh.

Chapter Eleven

The Trap

They took Kaushal into the foothills and installed him in a small village snuggling against a towering cliff. A monastery was built into the cliff's face.

"What religion is this?" said Kaushal.

"No religion," an old woman told him. "And all religions. Anyone can come here and seek enlightenment or pray. Even the Founder's followers. Most of our people are Followers of the Way, though."

"I thought Followers of the Way didn't need places to worship."

"We don't, but this is also our escape route. There is a cave entrance in the cliff wall at the monastery's rear. That cave winds around to a route through hills to a secret harbor where we can flee in boats, and on the way we're surrounded by rain forest where we can hide and harass our enemies."

Kaushal smiled. "That's where you'll all go when they come?"

She shook her head and gestured to the hills around them. "Our warriors will be there. We want them to assume you're in a village defended only by women and children. But we don't want to be in the crossfire. We'll use the cave if we have to."

It was a good plan. Lookouts would announce the arrival of the First Pilgrim's men. Other Wilders would let their enemies enter the village to search for Kaushal and then attack them.

Kaushal had a terrible thought. "What will they do to loyalists they capture?"

She shrugged. "We've never had prisoners before. It's always strike and run. The First Pilgrim's men often don't surrender because they expect their fate to be the same as what they dole out to us. They don't know anything else."

"You'll have to worry about it when some start surrendering," said Kaushal.

"For someone so young, you are wise. What would you suggest?"

"What do you do when one of your own commits murder?"

"It happens, and we banish them. There's an island not far away that's impossible to escape from by swimming due to the strong currents. Those banished can build boats, but we have patrols that destroy them. I'm afraid even our banished people would kill the First Pilgrim's men, though. The hatred burns in them even more."

"You have to find another island then."

***

"What are you doing here?" Kaushal said to Kifi when she entered the hut where he was staying.

"Some women will stay—the warriors among us. Others. We have to make it look good."

"And to protect me?"

"That, and to protect the retreat of the women and children and create another front. Others in the hills will come down and box them in. We'll squeeze from this direction. If things go badly, we'll disappear into the cave too. But let's try to look defenseless at first. Ezan's all set, by the way."

"For what?"

"Lounging with you in front and pretending you're lovers. It will make them assume you're distracted by pleasures of the flesh."

"I will be. You two would distract any man."

She blushed. "Don't enjoy our attentions in this temporary charade too much. We expect you to fight with us. Besides, Ezan has a husband."

"Maybe it should be only you tending to my romantic needs then?"

She smiled. "You wish. Tristan might think you're a stud, but you're just a boy-king to me."

"No chance, huh?"

She shook her head. "Not right now. Maybe the new king of Eden will have multiple wives like King Merson and King Breman, but that tradition is archaic and should disappear, the sooner the better. Let's ready our weapons."

***

Soldiers arrived two days later. Sentinels reported three troop carriers unloading about three hundred men and supplies at the wharf in the island's small harbor. The First Pilgrim's soldiers marched through the little town on their way upland, ignoring villagers who fled into the countryside.

Mountain Folk and Wilders were ready for them. First, they let the scouts see the idyllic village loaded with women and children. Ezan could be seen sharing a hammock with Kaushal, hugging and kissing him like he was the last man on Eden. From the corner of his eye, he spotted flashes from a mirror. Four long flashes, a short, and another long.

"You can stop now," said Kaushal. "The forward scouts are gone. It's time to take the women and children into the cave and prepare for battle."

She smiled at him. "Don't tell my husband, but I was enjoying that. I've never seduced a king before."

By then Kaushal had almost become accustomed to bare-breasted women, but both Ezan and Kifi's bosoms were distracting. Being with Ezan had been more than fun. His kilt hid his excitement, though.

"I'm not a king, and I don't want to be. We have to work on Tristan about that." He jumped from the hammock and uncovered their body armor and weapons, long knives and rifles one could fire with one hand but also steady with the other for sniper-like activity. "Let's prepare for battle."

Warriors remaining in the village were in hiding when the First Pilgrim's soldiers ascended the hill toward town. The hills around the town were filled with Wilders and Mountain Folk. The soldiers moved in mass. When they passed the first houses at the outskirts, some defenders in the hills opened fire while others swooped down on them.

The soldiers made a defensive formation against the attacks from the hills. That's when Kaushal and others in the village hit them from behind. The melee degenerated into fighting at close quarters where soldiers' longer rifles were a disadvantage. The clash of steel against steel echoed from the hills but only lasted for about five minutes. Twenty-three soldiers surrendered, their arms and legs bound irrespective of their wounds, and left to lie in the blistering sun.

Tristan approached Kaushal, who was holding his bloody long knife at his side. "Not bad for an entertainer, my boy. Let's take stock of our wounded and dead."

Three Wilders had died, but no Mountain Folk. Two Mountain Folk were wounded; one was Ezan. Both men and women started tending to wounded, even to the First Pilgrim's soldiers.

A youth came running up to Tristan. "We now have three new ships. The crewmembers surrendered. They wanted no part of a battle."

"I'm not surprised. They were all ashore in the pubs, right?"

"They'd left only two men on each boat. They surrendered too."

Tristan put a hand on the youth's shoulder. "Good running, lad. Go have some water before you die in this heat."

"What will Wilders do with the captives?" said Kaushal.

"Beats me. Not my problem." Tristan smiled. "Do you have a suggestion?"

Why do I feel this is a test? Kaushal made a suggestion along the lines of what he had discussed with the old woman.

"Sounds like a good idea. This archipelago has so many deserted islands that it's workable. I'll suggest it to Petro, but you own the idea. I won't take credit for good or bad ideas."

Kaushal watched him walk away. He didn't mind Tristan's first policy, but if he accepted a bad idea for good, shouldn't he share the blame? Kaushal was having a problem with some logical credos of the Way.

Chapter Twelve

Rest and Relaxation

The next three weeks were dedicated to rest and relaxation as weary and wounded recovered. They left the village where the temple was and moved toward the bay. It had a fine beach that became a playground. Informality was the rule as feasts, drinking and romantic liaisons became commonplace. It was a new experience for Kaushal.

He knew how to swim but didn't like the strong sun. When Ezan and Kifi stood in front of him, saltwater dripping from their nude bodies, he had to smile at them. *What man wouldn't smile?* He wanted to make love to them both, although they acted like twin sisters. Again he thought of Anju. Would she understand his lust?

"I should write a song about you two," he said.

Kifi took Ezan's face in her hands and kissed the younger woman on the lips. "And what would the lyrics say?" said Ezan. She tweaked Kifi's right nipple and watched it become aroused. "That you don't know how to enjoy a good party?"

The two women looked so much alike they could be sisters, but Ezan, the younger, was a bigger flirt. She rolled her breasts. "My friends here feel neglected. They ache for arousal by a man. I'll repeat Kifi's question. Don't you know we're celebrating?"

"I only know two gorgeous and hedonistic women are trying to seduce an innocent lad."

Kifi laughed. "We want you to enjoy the water, King Kaushal. Don't make a big deal of it."

She grabbed one hand, Ezan the other. Kaushal soon discovered the cool water was welcome relief from the hot sun. It was good for other things too. For the first time, he could forget about Anju and his lust for two Mountain Folk women.

***

It wasn't all fun and games, though. Some of them, Tristan's group included, would sit around a roaring campfire on the beach and develop plans.

"They won't ignore what happened here," Kifi said at one point. "They will come again. The First Pilgrim will assume Kaushal's organizing an opposition."

"The opposition is already organized," said Kaushal. "I've been lucky to become a part of it."

"True, we were organized before," said Tristan, "but you've become a catalyst, and they know it even if they don't understand it."

"Do they know who Kaushal is?" said one of the Wilder men, picking up the thread. "If not, it would be a tremendous advantage."

"I'd guess that Gol Kovlyn suspects," said Tristan. The thought a moment. "How well did you know this Anju?" he said to Kaushal. "Is she reliable?"

"I hope they didn't know about our friendship," said Kaushal. "She benefitted from my killing the king. That might put her under suspicion, but we were careful."

"But will she protect your secret?" said a Wilder woman.

"They'd have to know she possessed a secret before they tortured her," said Tristan.

Kaushal studied the man from the mountains. There had been no emotion in his voice. Had he seen so much torture he had become complacent about it? And what was his relation to those in orbit who monitored Eden?

"I hope she tells them her secret if there's even a hint of torture. She doesn't know much, after all. And I don't see how it would affect our cause either."

"They might assume she was an accomplice," said Kifi, "considering circumstances."

"Let's return to the main topic," said Tristan. "So far I've heard proposals that amount to bugs pestering a jonki. Perhaps useful to irritate the First Pilgrim, but not anywhere near a mortal blow. Any more ideas?"

***

"How much support do you have in Angels' Bay?" said Kaushal.

"A lot," said Tristan. "Even many First Tribesmen don't like the First Pilgrim's autocratic ways, and they know it can become worse with a new king." Kaushal watched the lithe Ezan throw two more logs on the fire. Tristan stared at the breakers. "We also have a presence in New Hope and Long Beach. What are you scheming?"

"A two-pronged attack on the castle complex," said Kaushal. "We can invade New Hope and push on to Long Beach and the capital to distract them from the south. Mountain Folk can attack from the mountains to pressure them from the north."

"And if they find out?" said Ezan. "They have spies everywhere. Some children spy on their parents because they're taught in schools to do that for the First Pilgrim. More than one parent was beheaded because his son or daughter spied on him."

Tristan nodded. "That's our gravest danger. There are also those who would turn us in for money because there's so much poverty. I would worry about flyovers too. The flotilla is smaller with every passing year, but they still do air surveillance. How can we hide the massive troop buildups?"

Kaushal shrugged. "Our success here showed subterfuge is our friend. We need to put our heads together to devise a plan that combines cunning with force. You asked for something beyond bugs pestering a jonki, but I bet if thousands attack him all at once, he'll feel more than pestered."

"Most herd animals are female," said Kifi with a smile, "but you have a valid point. A swarm will make a jonki go crazy and run for water to escape all the bugs."

Tristan also smiled at that.

Chapter Thirteen

Education of a Warrior

The R&R period ended and Kaushal's education began. Wilders and Mountain Folk started training him to be a warrior. He wasn't a violent person, but they lived in a violent world. Kifi and Tristan taught him hand-to-hand combat. Ezan and others taught him about weapons. Swords, knives, and pistols were used for short range; spears, bows and arrows, and rifles for long. They taught him how to weave body armor from tough vines found on the mountain slopes and cure hides to finish them off and make leather belts and scabbards. He learned how to find water and shield himself from the elements.

The most fun to be had was learning how to sail. Wilders used every type of boat imaginable, but they tended to use oars and sails more than motorized vessels because fuel had to be stolen. Kaushal's favorite vehicle was a long sailboat made from a hollowed-out trunk of a tree with two thinner, hollowed-out branches used alongside for stability. They were fast. Kaushal loved skimming over the waves inside one.

Along with sailing came swimming and diving.

"You need to show me how to do that," he said as Ezan and Kifi surfaced with netted bags full of wriggling creatures.

They were anchored in the bay. Ezan and Kifi were contributing to future dinners. The creatures would be smoked, salted, and stored between leaves. Kifi shielded her eyes from the water's glare to look at him. She bobbed up in the water and pointed down to her waist. He tried to ignore her breasts and focus on the belt she wore, her only clothing.

"We need to make you a stone-weighted belt. It's easier to get to the bottom. The faster the better. We don't have tanks. We'll prepare the belt this afternoon and tomorrow you can try."

"Tanks?"

"Diving equipment," said Ezan, climbing into the boat and shaking off the water. It was a process that went from head to toes; her bronzed skin flashed in the sun. "Fishermen in the shore's big cities use them so they can stay under for a long time. We're lucky to manage four or five minutes."

"You need compressed air for tanks. Pumps need fuel." Kifi frowned. "Even if we had tanks, we couldn't use them. We need what fuel we have for boats that need it."

But Kaushal was already considering another idea. One side of the castle was considered invincible because it was at the top of rugged cliffs. But the cliffs were only five-men tall.

***

That night it was Kifi's turn. At first, Kaushal had thought about Anju and felt guilty, but both Kifi and Ezan had laughed and told him it was part of his education. After trying to satisfy them both, he had suggested they take turns. That cooled things off a bit—the two together were too inventive about what they could do with his body and theirs.

He'd queried Tristan about it.

"That's what men and women do," the Mountain Folk's spiritual leader said. "Women are attracted to strong, young men, and vice versa. At first, it's just sexual heat, but later it mellows and becomes something called love. No one understands it beyond the universal necessity of biological organisms to reproduce in order to preserve the species. Humans are biological creatures, after all."

"Mountain Folk and Wilders have few inhibitions, but you don't ever engage in the fun."

"I'm more of a spiritual person. I understand the theory but not the practice. So I can't make many good suggestions." He smiled. "Except, don't let them wear you out."

"What about Ezan's husband?"

Tristan nodded. "Ah, the concept of fidelity." He paused. "Some human beings create rules to live by where infidelity is considered immoral. The Founder preached abstinence until marriage. Many people on Paradise and Eden have found such rules hypocritical considering the hedonistic nature of the upper echelons of society. Anju was going to be forced to marry her uncle, for example. Not incest, but a rape sanctioned by the king and the First Pilgrim." He shrugged. "Do what you feel is right. But remember, some people might expect a future king to be a bit promiscuous."

"How about respecting a king who's not?"

"I understand your hesitation. Did you ever sleep with Anju?"

"No. I respected her."

"And you don't respect Kifi or Ezan?"

"They're different. They're older, experienced women, and they came after me. And I do respect them too. And I'm attracted to them. That's part of the problem."

"A king often feels alone on his throne," said Tristan, "but a king who respects and serves his subjects has won the most important battle."

"What's that?"

"Realizing he's no better than and no different from anyone else. There's no battle more important for a human being to face. And all troubles in human history can be traced to human beings who didn't win that battle."

"You're quite the philosopher at times."

Tristan smiled. "I do my best. Following the Way makes it easier."

***

After a few months, those training him told a bronzed Kaushal he was ready to participate in any plans they might develop against the First Pilgrim and the royal court. Word had arrived that a new king was now on the throne. As usual, King Farben, second cousin of the murdered king, was the First Pilgrim's puppet. He was also Kaushal's age, malleable and much more interested in the good life than affairs of state, although it was rumored he enjoyed blood and violence.

"Maybe we should wait until the First Pilgrim passes on and convince this young man to make amends to his people," said Ezan one night around the campfire.

"By the Founder, woman," said one Wilders man, "you assume you can win the heart of any boy-king!"

No one could see Kaushal's blush in the darkness surrounding the dying embers of the fire.

"By the Founder, man," said Ezan, "everyone knows no woman can win your black heart."

There were laughs.

"If he has a heart," said Kifi. "What's your opinion, Kaushal?"

"It is people's minds we must win if we are going to accomplish our goals. We must act or we will get soft. This idyllic existence makes the real problems of Eden seem far away, but that's only a state of mind."

"So, do you great philosophers have a battle plan?" said the Wilders man.

"We do," said Petro, who had returned from Big Island three days before. "It's a variant on what Kaushal proposed.

87

Samos will explain it. We have a lot of preparation ahead of us, to say the least."

They all listened intently. When Samos finished, Kaushal winked at Tristan.

"Does that meet with your approval?"

"It's a good plan," said Tristan. "Not everyone has to participate, but all must be in agreement. Kindri already has the agreement of Mountain Folk. Now we must seek the agreement from the remainder of the Wilders. Petro?"

"I'm sure they'll agree. We're tired of our puny raids on Angels' Bay. And soldiers and spies are improving all the time as they exploit and abuse all but nobles in the First Pilgrim's court—or should I say, King Farben's court now?"

"It's always been the First Pilgrim's court, even back on Paradise," said Tristan.

Kaushal wondered about that. It wasn't the first time he had heard something mentioned that was forgotten history to many people on Eden. Had Tristan come from Paradise too? *And how old is he?*

Chapter Fourteen

The Campaign against Farben Begins

Agreement among Wilders came soon. Kifi and Ezan returned to the Mountain Folk to help coordinate the northern front. Kaushal and Tristan stayed behind to help organize the Wilders' attack. Their first target? New Hope, a much smaller and compact city on Hope Bay compared to the sprawling capital, Angel's Bay.

Tired of logistics, Kaushal made his habitual visit to Tristan's tent.

"You are still curious about the tablets?" said Tristan. He was sitting in a lotus position, hands open and resting on his knees but saw his protégé eying the electronics. "You have an obsession."

"You took my toys. I guarded them with my life. Isn't it reasonable to ask what you've done with them?"

Tristan sighed. "Youth is always inquisitive, I suppose. Can't you take my word that you have no need to know at this moment? We have other things on our minds, after all."

"And can't you understand those things were my only tie to Anju? What's become of her? Don't we have spies in the court?"

"Not enough. Two were beheaded last week. One was a person you were fond of."

"Who?" Tristan told him. Kaushal sank to his knees. "The old sous-chef Alis was a spy?" Kaushal sensed the rising vomit, jumped up, and dashed out.

"Come, sit," said Tristan, when he returned. "The First Pilgrim petitioned King Farben for clemency for Alis, but the king denied it. He enjoys watching heads fall, but the First Pilgrim probably enjoys a good meal more. And I do have information for you about Anju. King Farben wants to marry her. It looks like you have competition."

Kaushal slammed his right fist into his left palm. "I need to kill another king."

"An emotional response and perhaps justified, but keep your head about you. You might receive your wish if you're patient—Farben is a lazy lout and incapable of taking you on—but right now our plans take priority. Do you understand?" Kaushal nodded. "Good. Now I have something else to discuss. Do you know the spaceport on the outskirts of Angels' Bay?"

"I know where it is, yes. It's been awhile since I've been there. It's been abandoned since the First Tribe usurped power. Only relics remain. Why?"

"Smart tacticians have a Plan B as well as a Plan A, so listen closely."

***

They trickled into New Hope by twos and threes, their small boats making round trips between Southlands and city. Once there, Wilders hid among sympathizers in the city. Others unloaded weapons and ammunition and hid those.

Unbeknownst to soldiers stationed in the barracks overlooking Hope Bay, the population of New Hope tripled within a week. When Wilders overran the barracks, known sympathizers of the new king and the First Pilgrim were captured and imprisoned. Three soldiers and two sympathizers died. One of the Wilders suffered a broken arm when he slipped on a wet spot in the barracks. New Hope belonged to Wilders, and the capital didn't even know it.

"We've increased the number of people we can throw at Long Beach," said Kaushal, now at ease in a pub enjoying an ale.

"They're motivated," said Petro, "but we have a problem."

"They're not trained," said Tristan with a nod. "We can spend a few days with them, but I'd like to use most of them to control things here after we leave for Long Beach."

"What about soldiers who expressed interest in joining us?" said Kaushal.

"Do you trust them?" said Petro.

"Not yet," said Tristan. "Maybe with time. That's another reason to depend more on our original people. Besides, we don't have enough ships."

"Will Long Beach know we're coming?"

"They will if we dawdle and spend time trying to train locals into a fighting force," said Petro. "The word's bound to get out. I say we move on soon."

Tristan nodded. "Let's rest another day and travel during the night."

"Same tactics?" said Kaushal.

"No. We have a schedule to keep. Stealth is still our friend, though."

Kaushal smiled. They had to hit Angels' Bay from the south right after Mountain Folk hit it from the north. In a sense, it didn't matter whether they could hold New Hope or Long Beach, as long as the capital and the castle fell.

***

The soldier on the wharf put a chaw of sopo in his mouth to kill the boredom and stared at the inky water. At least he hadn't drawn this posting on Founder's Day. He could revel with the rest and sleep in. Tonight he would have to suffer with Dexo. *Where is that SOB?*

Those guarding Long Beach for the First Pilgrim and King Farben were lowly soldiers, not the elite Royal Guards. Their training hadn't been as complete, and they were less motivated. The farther from the capital, the less they cared about what happened there. Like soldiers in New Hope, they lived a less stressful life. The soldier was thankful for that.

Four sentries were assigned intersecting circuits along the docks and wharves. Long Beach, known for its long stretch of sand where rich elites came to play in the sun and waves, was also the most important port on this side of Big Island. It was deeper than the port at Angels' Bay and serviced ships trading among many archipelagoes in that area of Eden. They traded with some Southlands islands, making a lot of profit even while paying tribute to Wilders pirates.

Little wealth trickled down to the poor, a class that included the soldier. Being in the service of the King and First Pilgrim was better than being a thief or pirate, from life expectancy to riches.

The sentry waited at the point where he and Dexo should cross paths, puzzled and peering both ways along the docks. The only noise came from the gentle lapping of waves on the shore. He was getting nervous. Dexo was a good soldier and not one to miss a round.

The sentry heard a psst! behind him, turned, and saw a woman standing nearby, waggling her tits at him. He smiled, but the smile disappeared as a strong arm from behind reached around his neck. He struggled, but the lack of oxygen soon put him down.

"Two more," Kaushal said to Kifi.

***

After another fifteen minutes, docks were clear and boats started to arrive.

Almost all Wilders troops hid in the outskirts of Long Beach, but some took the places of sentries at the docks. The barracks nearer town center became the next target.

Due to the size of the port, Long Beach had a larger contingent of soldiers. Casualties on both sides were more numerous, but by afternoon Kaushal was on a high rampart with a view of Hope Bay on one side and Dragon's Mountain on the other, the ancient volcano wafting wispy trails of white smoke into the clear blue sky.

"The view is spectacular," said Petro, "and shows we have to do better than the king and the court in protecting our home planet. A large percentage of wells in Long Beach are contaminated by sewer effluent, for example, and the rest is dumped into the bay."

"The same is true in Angels' Bay," said Kaushal. "When it's high noon with soaring temperatures, you want to plug your nose, the stench is so bad. My father had plans. He knew that increasing population would only make it worse."

"He had good qualities," said Petro. "Do you recognize the bad ones?"

Kaushal shrugged. "He was a product of his times and culture. With time, he could have done many things, but the First Tribe's invasion ended all those possibilities. We need to make revolutionary changes now to counteract the First Tribe's damages to the planet and its peoples."

"Well spoken, my friend. Shall we go below? Tristan has news."

They walked down steep stone stairs into the barracks' bowels. Even through the walls, he could hear moans of the wounded soldiers, both Wilders and king's soldiers. There wasn't much they could do for them. Healthcare in the provinces, even this near Angels' Bay, was minimal and of poor quality. Only rich elites had competent care, and they and their doctors were under arrest now and not to be trusted.

"We have word from the mountains," said Tristan as the two entered. "Everything is ready for the final push toward the capital."

"As bad as today was," said Petro, "it will be trivial compared to the battle facing us. King Farben and the First Pilgrim will throw everything at us as they try to survive. Soldiers guarding the residential areas of the rich elites and the castle are mean and well-fed and will not show mercy."

"Nor are they stupid." Kaushal smiled. "But not as smart as we are."

"Don't be too cocky," said Tristan. "Your escape was part skill and part luck. Remember how Kifi captured you?"

"I'll accept your rebuke, but I have more skills now."

"And more muscles," said Petro. "May the Founder smile upon us."

Kaushal frowned. "Don't bring the Founder into this discussion. We have to realize these religious trappings are only a means to control the masses. 'You'll have your reward in the arms of the Founder,' they say, but when we're dead, we're dead, and when we're alive, the Founder's arms strangle us."

The older man took a step forward. "That kind of blasphemy isn't productive," said Petro.

Kaushal held up a hand to stop the advance. "Get with the program, old man. We only have one life to live, so we'd better make the most of it."

"Enough!" said Tristan. "I might agree with you, Kaushal, but it's irrelevant. The goal is to have a social structure that recognizes and respects all belief systems, and to end this lunacy of shoving someone's belief system down the throats of non-believers."

Petro shrugged but nodded. "I can understand your rage against the Founder, but he isn't the person who brought all these ills to Eden. We have a common goal, at least for now, so let's stick to it, for the good of all of us."

***

After the meeting to discuss tactics and the others left to rest for the final battle, Tristan pulled Kaushal aside.

"This is not the time to debate philosophy with Petro or anyone else for that matter," he said.

"Aren't you worried we'll replace tyrants in Angels' Bay with new ones like Petro?" said Kaushal. "I'll have none of that."

Tristan nodded. "There's bound to be some instability if we succeed, and horrible repercussions if we don't. Do you remember Plan B?"

"Are you being pessimistic? It's gone well so far."

"Provincial outposts are complacent. The worst soldiers are sent here. You saw Long Beach was more difficult than New Hope. Angels' Bay will be far worse. No matter the outcome, many will die. Friends you have made might draw their last breaths, either on the battlefield or in executions. You have to prepare for that."

"What choice do I have?"

"You can return to the mountains right now and live among Mountain Folk, the ones who are left. They'll do you no harm."

"But I will have failed them, Wilders, and you. Some choice."

Tristan smiled. "There is always a choice. Do you want to meditate?"

Kaushal nodded. He dropped into a lotus position. Tristan placed a hand on Kaushal's forehead. It was cold but comforting.

"The Way is arduous for all those who would follow it," the Mountain Folk leader intoned.

Chapter Fifteen

The Battle for Angels' Bay

The advance from the south to Angel's Bay was also a two-pronged attack. One group moved northwest from Long Beach across the coastal plain straight for the capital. The other group went by sea to the bluffs at bay's end and approached more from the east. Mountain Folk hit first, descending from the foothills, running over the small contingent guarding the old spaceport and moving into the conurbation to the north of the city.

Kaushal and Petro were with the sea force, Tristan with Wilders coming from Long Beach. Kaushal knew Kifi and Ezan would be with Mountain Folk.

It wasn't too hot and some fog was blowing off the river. The cool mist felt refreshing in the heat of battle.

We are going to paint this idyllic landscape with blood, thought Kaushal. From what he'd seen of Eden so far during his adventures outside castle walls, the planet should have been called Paradise. It had everything men and women needed to live in peace and prosperity. *Why must we fight?* He looked skywards and thought of the surveillance ship in orbit. *How spectacular their view must be!*

The more he saw, the less he believed Nut had bequeathed them the planet. *If there be gods, this cannot be the work of only one.* But Tristan had taught him the mysteries of the Way. The Universe was bigger than any realm of the gods. It was and would forever be—difficult to understand, but it made sense.

He tapped the side of his head, touching the empty socket out of habit and for luck. What the people called magic was only technology. It's created by sentient beings, not gods. Petro didn't grasp that. Speaking of the devil...

"It's a good day for fighting," Petro said to Kaushal.

Kaushal approached the older man. He was kneeling, eyes glued to the screen of a message tablet. Kaushal helped him to his feet. Petro stood tall, still holding the tablet with one hand but raising his long knife high with the other for all to see. They were waiting for a message from the Mountain Folk's advance guard. Both Kaushal and Tristan had tablets. The message came. They moved forward.

People in the outskirts of Angels' Bay to the river's south offered little resistance. Most were impoverished Second Tribesmen and First Tribe malcontents who were happy to see Wilders. Many joined their ranks. Women and children followed to care for the wounded.

As they approached the river, they met hundreds of soldiers fleeing Mountain Folk on the other side. Now those soldiers had little choice—surrender or fight. Most fought; many died. The wave of Wilders moved across the bridge, joined Mountain Folk, and turned toward the castle. The other group of Wilders attacked the castle defenses from the north.

They were a half kilometer from the castle when the tide started to turn. They had met the elite troops of the king's Royal Guard. Squads of loyalist sharpshooters wreaked havoc with their long rifles. Other squads with pistols and long knives moved forward. Mountain Folk and Wilders couldn't match their weaponry or fighting skill.

Kaushal saw Petro fall and rushed toward him. His blank eyes stared at the sky as brain matter oozed from the bullet hole in his forehead.

"Kaushal, watch out!"

He pivoted and impaled a soldier with his long knife. He sheathed it and started firing with his pistol. He had to drop it when one of their own arrows pierced his arm. He broke it off almost at the end but couldn't remove the barbed tip.

He heard the message tablet buzz. A message from Tristan. "Plan B!" it said.

Kaushal looked around. He couldn't see Tristan, but he assumed the Mountain Folk leader was there somewhere. He spotted Kifi about five meters distant. She was battling one Guard but another approached her rear with a long knife. He grabbed his own with his left hand and threw it. The soldier pitched forward; Kaushal's knife had skewered him in the back below the shoulder blade.

"It's a good day to die!" said Kifi, acknowledging him.

Plan B! Plan B! Kaushal found Petro's weighty scimitar and fell back, working his way through the battleground and breaking into the clear. He started to run and dodge, leaving a trail of blood from his arm. *They'll think I'm a coward!* But he'd made a promise to Tristan. He hoped the Mountain Folk leader would survive and tell everyone that.

The Guards had abandoned the old spaceport. There was nothing really to guard there after all. He pushed through a junkyard of derelict ships until he located the one he wanted. He brushed aside years of refuse and drax feces. The entry code was simple: 31416. An entry hatch opened, and he climbed in, shutting the hatch behind him. The stale and moldy air reminded him of a tomb. But this was no tomb. *But will it be?*

He pushed aside old tablets and what looked like uniforms, sat in the pilot's chair, and punched in the code again. The ship seemed to shake itself awake as it rose from the dead.

Part Three.

The ITUIP Protocol

With the Protocol, we often tie our hands when dealing with planets not belonging to ITUIP. As crewmembers of an exploratory ship, we often find cultural aberrations in unofficial colonies we thought didn't exist. It's surprising the variety we find, from peaceful and rustic nomads to oppressive, fundamentalist regimes. The only good words I can say about this situation are that it makes for some interesting adventures.

—Carlos Obregon, medical officer (ret) of the starship *Brendan*

Chapter Sixteen

Skywatch

Captain Rezo Banton heard three beeps, rolled over in his bunk, and grabbed his com device. Some slept with the damn things plugged into the sides of their head. He couldn't. For one thing, he was bald and had no hair to cushion it. For another, one of his erogenous zones was behind the ears. His wife, who was in engineering when she was on duty, looked at him and raised an eyebrow.

She knows my erogenous zones well. The Way is good to me. He raised a finger to his lips and smiled as he tasted her. Smiled for her to put her at ease.

"Go back to sleep. This is likely nothing important." He subvocalized to contact the caller with his device. "This had better be good, Yago!"

He knew the threat was meaningless. Yago didn't apologize much. Their relationship was more one of mutual respect.

"There's a ship ascending from Eden on an orbital intercept trajectory. ID beacon says it's Tristan's old clunker. Docking soon. How shall we receive it?"

"Considering you woke Diana and me, I'm inclined to shoot the damn thing down. But see if you can raise whoever's flying it. It can't be empty. Not from down there. I'll be there in a bit."

He managed to close all his fasteners on the way to the bridge. It was more important to don the slippers that provided enough traction to keep Newton's first or second law from killing him in the microgravity field as he hurried through the ship.

When he arrived he stood with hands on hips and surveyed his crew on the bridge for a moment before Yago had a chance to detect his presence. He was proud of them. They were a good bunch, all of them. And on this mission, they had to have patience. The Way taught that for those who followed it, of course, but others were patient too. That involved both character and training. ITUIP's exploratory ships spent about ninety percent of their subjective time waiting while the ship went from point A to B. But only on surveillance missions were they required to spend it long at point B.

He was a small, muscular man. He had stopped his aging process when the first gray came in behind his ears, but out of convenience still chose to shave his head. Unlike other spacefaring Humans, he didn't have to do that, at least not often. While others did so or even had their follicles removed, including his wife, he kept the customs of his home planet.

Now he was in a bit of a disarray. The wakeup call had disturbed his morning ritual. He liked having some time to do a light breakfast with his wife before they went about their different duties. She was less insistent about that than he was—he thought her love was shared between him and the ship—but he maintained the morning ritual, no matter how morning was defined.

"Captain on the bridge!" said Yago Cofa, who had been in command when he awoke Rezo.

"At ease, people," said Rezo from habit, but they were already at ease—that was the way he ran his ship. "Any contact with that shuttle?"

"No sir," said Lala Helf, who was now com expert on the bridge. She looked a lot like his wife and for a good reason. They were more than sisters—they were clones—but their different personalities made it easy for Rezo to tell them apart. Lala was more of a flirt, for example, but his wife didn't seem to mind. "I can't raise anyone. For all we know, it's empty."

"Com might be inactive," said Yago. "Can it be Tristan?"

Yago was tall and angular, with sunken cheeks accentuated by his almost perpetual frown. He could pass for a fasting priest. That matched another duty: he was one Guide to the Way onboard. Rezo used them all for his meditation sessions.

"Who knows? Just our luck. In a week our replacement would be here, and we would be on our way to have a nice shore leave somewhere. Can't our AI link with the shuttle's?"

"The shuttle appears to be on automatic pilot. We only know the escape sequence was initiated." Yago pointed to two other big screens that accepted satellite feeds from around Eden. They showed the capital, Angels' Bay. "A big battle is raging below."

"Who's winning?" said Rezo. There was always violence. Edenites seemed to thrive on it as much as food and sex. He caught Lala smiling at him. *Does she know I'm thinking about Edenite harems?* His wife often seemed to read his mind, often completing his sentences.

"The tide has turned in favor of the new king's Royal Guards," she said. "Insurgents are in retreat for the most part."

"In other words, that damn First Pilgrim is winning," said Rezo. "I sure wish we could help those folk. Let's see what we can do for whoever's on that shuttle."

***

The shuttle bay on the ITUIP explorer ship *Zheng He* was small, but the arriving shuttle entered and landed alongside the ship's other two with room to spare. The recent arrival seemed like a relic from a past era next to the newer and larger vehicles.

Rezo, hands on hips again, stared for a bit and then shook his head. "That's a damn rust bucket. How long ago did we send Tristan down there?"

"Right after the First Tribe's invasion of Eden," said one crewmember.

"You mean when that stupid Second Tribe's king gave them refuge? What was that fool thinking?" The First Tribe had already shown their stripes by leaving many of their numbers to freeze or starve on Paradise. That was long ago. "OK. And it's been oxidizing there ever since? I'm amazed it still flies. Anyone know how to enter one of these old boats?"

"Everything should still be on automatic," said another crewmember.

"You mean under the ship's own AI control? That's not much comfort. Its code is likely older."

But the hatch opened. Weapons were readied. A young man crawled out, stared at them a bit, and raised his hands.

"I come in peace. I mean you no harm."

He spoke one dialect of the locals, the Second Tribe version; both corresponded to corrupted Standard, antiques like the ship. The *Zheng He*'s AI whispered the translation into everyone's com device.

"Lower your weapons," said Rezo. "We'll take him at his word for now. Doc, are you listening? We need you. This fellow's injured. He has half a damn arrow stuck in his arm near the shoulder."

Rezo made a sweeping motion with his hand, inviting the newcomer to come his way. The stranger walked beside him and others fell in behind.

He noted the young man looked strong and had a commanding presence even though he was wounded. He also looked familiar.

"You are the watchers," the stranger said. "I saw you on a wall screen in one of the secret rooms in Starlight Castle. Where are the Rangers?" Rezo shook his index finger, used both hands to make like he was tapping soil into a flower bed, and then pointed to the com device in back of his ear. The visitor understood his message. "You can understand me, but I can't understand you. How will we communicate?"

Rezo pointed again to the device and made the same tapping motion with the hands. He then motioned for the Edenite to continue walking with him. He stumbled a few times in the microgravity, but Rezo caught him. They ended at the infirmary.

The newcomer backed away from the huge, furry humanoid who approached him. He pointed with his ebony hand toward the arrow.

Rezo reached up and put his arm around his ship's doctor. "Hamil's a Tali. Tali. They're called Tali. Our crew is composed of Humans, Rangers, and Talis." Rezo pointed to himself. "Human." Then the medic. "Tali."

"Ranger?"

Rezo made the tapping motion again. "All in good time."

The doctor invited him to sit on a table and began examining the wound. Rezo and the others retreated. The captain remained behind in the corridor outside the infirmary, sending the others in the security detail back to their other duties. The stranger was docile enough.

Rezo was trying to remember where he'd seen this visitor before. He needed to go through the logs. They had centuries' worth of data on the planet. The ship's AI would help him sort it out. *I need a memory rejuvenation. I've been doing this for too long.*

***

"Any idea who he is?" said Rezo, still pondering the stranger's ID in the corridor outside the infirmary.

"He must be someone in Tristan's confidence," said Yago from the bridge. "Otherwise, how would he have the code? We're working on an ID."

"He could have stolen the code from Tristan. But it might not matter. The arrow implies he was involved in the battle. Tristan might be too. What's it look like below?"

"A rout. The good guys had a great strategic plan, but the king's Royal Guard was too well equipped and prepared. They'll reorganize now and move to retake Long Beach and New Hope, killing all the rebels."

"They control them now? That must stick in King Farben's throat as well as anger the First Pilgrim big time. Are any who were doing battle with the Guards escaping?"

"Those who can. The Royal Guards are killing the wounded, I'm afraid. They aren't taking prisoners, so the Second Tribe's casualties are horrendous. I watched some—"

"Spare me the gory details. We're dealing with savages from a barbarian culture here. Feral Humans can be more bloodthirsty than any other sentient beings, and they'll often revert to savagery. It's in our genetic makeup, I'm afraid."

"We were all that way. It's an ancient and chronic mental illness. If you consider the Roman Empire, for example—"

"Don't give me all that historical crap. Discover who this guy is and keep me posted on events below."

Rezo saw Hamil crook a black, leathery finger at him and returned to the infirmary.

"Our young guest is now communicating," said the doctor after Rezo followed him inside. "He already had the implant. It wasn't a modern one, so I had to be a little creative with some microsurgery."

The Edenite tapped the plug in his ear and another device resting on his hairy chest. It hung by a thin, transparent cord.

"What's your name, lad?" said Rezo.

"Kaushal. Tristan sent me."

"Figured as much. Was Tristan involved in that battle?" Kaushal nodded. "Figured that too. The damn fool can't leave well enough alone, but he's a good monitor."

Kaushal looked surprised. "Was he spying on us?"

"Not you in particular. He's been observing everything there for a long time. He kept us informed about what was happening. My guess is he was working with you. That's not being a spy, but a busybody, even if he worked with you."

"He's a watcher?" Kaushal looked surprised.

"Of sorts. Monitor is a better name for us. I have some better ones for him, but we needed someone there with his special characteristics. Come with me, lad."

Kaushal bowed to Hamil. "I want to thank you for mending my arm. I must apologize for my initial reaction. We only know non-Humans from the frescoes. You're much more imposing in person."

The Tali waved his right hand in a circle and with one leathery finger pointed at himself.

Will Kaushal know that's his acknowledgment of the apology? Damn AIs don't translate body language well.

"Frescoes?" said Rezo.

"In a secret room in the castle. I know more about Starlight Castle than most First Tribesmen in the royal court. I was an entertainer there."

"We'll continue your story in the meeting room. This place stinks like a hospital."

"It is a hospital," said Hamil. "A small one, but still a hospital. You should remember that from when you acquired that disease on Crowley's World."

"Yeah, yeah, you saved my ass. And kept the rest of the crew from acquiring that plague. You're a regular Obregon, my friend, but don't let it go to your head."

As they walked out, Rezo winked at Hamil and added a suggestion. "Process that DNA for ID," he said in the Tali's guttural language. Rezo had ordered the ship's AI to translate only Human Standard into Kaushal's mother tongue. For DNA tests, they didn't have access to many records, just the ones Tristan and others had created, but some primitives might object to such a search. Something about a belief one's bodily fluids being sacred gifts from the Almighty Ra. Or was it Isis? He couldn't keep all their damn deities straight.

**

Rezo sat at one end of the conference table, Kaushal at his side.

"How did you come to meet Tristan?" said Rezo.

Kaushal told his story but eliminated some important details. He admitted killing King Breman and fleeing Starlight Castle.

"Let me interrupt for a moment," said Rezo. "Do you know why it's called Starlight Castle?"

"My fa—King Merson christened it in that manner. That's all I know."

"Merson was an amateur astronomer. He loved looking at the stars. There must be another secret room somewhere that you didn't discover because we know he had an observatory. He told Tristan that."

"I can't believe he knew Tristan? The man looks only a bit older than I am."

"He's a health fanatic," said Rezo with a shrug. "But go on with your story."

Kaushal continued.

"So you helped Tristan organize Mountain Folk and Wilders. Interesting."

"Mountain Folk were already organized. Wilders had a more chaotic organization but joined in the common cause. We convinced them. They're related to Mountain Folk and are mostly from the Second Tribe."

"We? Do you mean Tristan and you?" Kaushal nodded. "Why would they listen to you? Did they assume killing the king qualified you to be a leader? That's a stretch."

"In any case, we organized and we attacked. We all thought it was a good plan. And we prepared it over many months. It should have succeeded."

"From what I know, it was succeeding. Those elite soldiers were too prepared and well-equipped for you. That's too bad and not knowing that your only failure. But Tristan should have known that. Why did he send you here? Why didn't he come himself?"

"Plan B requires I be here and he remain on Eden."

By the time he finished, Rezo was impressed with their Plan B. But it presented a problem. *Will ITUIP approve it?*

***

Yago took Kaushal on a tour of the ship while Rezo returned to confer with Hamil.

The two first visited the control room similar to the one Anju and Kaushal had seen on wall screens in their secret room. Every person on the bridge had a specialized job, but

Yago explained that most could manage to take over different duties if the situation required.

Kaushal found the blinking, colored lights on instruments mesmerizing. At that moment, though, the huge screens were dark. *Don't they want me to see what's going on below? I already know my people are in trouble. What can it hurt?*

He knew some of the crew's secrecy was only because he didn't have the knowledge needed to understand what was going on. Although he didn't believe in magic, the experience was magical. But he also knew they were hiding things from him.

"Do you people park here in orbit and watch us?" said Kaushal, after leaving the bridge.

"Yes, but it's not much fun," said Yago. "That's why we take turns. We used to do the same for Earth after the Tali invasion. In that case, it was Humans versus Talis, but still the same idea—we were monitoring hostilities between them on the planet. In your case, it's a bit more difficult. Two sets of feral Humans are going at each other."

"Feral? We're not beasts."

"You do beastly things to each other. Same difference." Kaushal thought about that as he followed Yago into a small room with cabinets covering all the walls except for some strange appliances. "This is a small galley. We have several of these onboard. There's a bigger communal hall too. If you ever become hungry, find one and chow down."

"ITUIP is a union of many planets separated by great distances. How does this ship manage to travel that far?"

"I'll have to ask the captain's wife to give you the quick synopsis. She's an engineer. Non-technicals call it faster-than-light or FTL propulsion. That's wrong. Scooting around Eden's solar system, this ship isn't a lot speedier than ones that explored Earth's solar system long ago. For now, think of moving from solar system to solar system as a mathematical trick. The ship skips through many possible universes so the speed of light in this one isn't a factor."

"Light doesn't have infinite speed?"

Yago smiled. "You have some interesting holes in your education. Don't worry. You'll catch up. This is the Rangers' ring." They approached a huge toroidal structure as tall as Kaushal. Yago peered through a small window. "Two of our friends are in there now, exercising."

Kaushal peered inside the tube and saw two Rangers cavorting in the swirling waters. They looked like the creatures in the frescoes.

"Looks like fun," he said.

"Yes, there's that, but they also need it to survive. Low g-forces don't bother them so much, but they need to swim in water every so often. But this is the rec area. On the other side, you'd find a gym for other crewmembers. It still takes a while to dance through multiverses. That's a big problem, by the way. Ships like this are still the fastest way to carry messages back and forth between members of ITUIP and beyond. Come along. I have something interesting to show you."

Kaushal followed Yago into a lounge reminding the Edenite of similar rooms in the castle. A wide window allowed them to look at the planet. Kaushal saw the archipelagoes of his home and could pick out Angels' Bay. Beyond the shimmering atmosphere's edge, he saw stars.

"It's beautiful."

"Yes, it is, and it looks a lot more hospitable than Paradise. Looks are deceiving. Too bad you folks can't get along down there."

"My people didn't pick the fight. The First Tribe, led by the First Pilgrim, did. They schemed and took over Eden. Now we're just trying to survive."

Yago nodded. "We know. But we can't do anything about it. The ITUIP Protocol won't let us."

"I have to change that then."

Chapter Seventeen

A Change in Plans

"I can't figure this kid out," said Rezo. "He's wise beyond his years. He and Tristan make quite a pair." He explained Plan B to Hamil. "What do you think?"

"ITUIP will never approve. It violates the Protocol."

"If Brent Mueller had obeyed that Protocol, Dimitri Negrini would be ruling the galaxy as emperor by now. Any rule can have exceptions."

Hamil nodded. "Perhaps if the young Human appears before the General Council?"

"Why would they listen to him?"

"He's Prince Kaushal, King Merson's son. I confirmed that. We had plenty of his blood samples from the arrow extraction. We also had the old king's DNA on file, taken before the First Tribe took over."

"I'll be damned. He's a survivor then. He said he was an entertainer in the court. They couldn't have known he was a Second Tribe royal; he'd be dead otherwise."

"If you access one of Tristan's reports—" Hamil gave the file number for reference— "you'll see he was successful as an entertainer. That's how he was able to kill the First Tribe's king. But he knew his way around the castle from when he was a child. His father might have built all the secret passageways and such to amuse his children. Or himself."

Kaushal's background cleared up, Rezo lost interest in the royal lineage. Monarchies and theocracies were institutions unheard of in modern secular societies. He changed the topic.

"There would have been fewer casualties if Tristan swapped Plan A and B," he said with a growl. "What he's done also borders on illegal, but we can't prosecute him."

"Tristan is respected, but he doesn't lead Mountain Folk, and Wilders have their own leaders."

"But they followed Kaushal?"

"A team effort, if Lala's intel is correct. I'm afraid Tristan might be one of those casualties. We've received no more reports since the battles started. Yago is piecing together a complete story from our ship's SAR and satellite images."

"We'll have to debrief the prince. It would be useful to know whether Tristan survived."

"There is a problem. We have two versions of Plan B. Kaushal assumes you're going to bring our firepower to bear on the king's warriors. He's eager to lead us into battle."

"Why would Tristan give him that idea?"

"He didn't. He only told Kaushal we might help. Kaushal imagined what that help might be within his social context. Considering his violent history, it's a reasonable assumption."

"We'll have to set him straight. The most we can do now is to let him try to convince the Council to make an exception to the Protocol and lift the quarantine, but I'm sure they won't want to start sending heavy modern weapons in to blast a primitive planet's bad guys."

"You need a Plan C then."

***

They waited until their replacements arrived. After turning over monitoring to the new surveillance crew, the *Zheng He* left orbit to begin its voyage toward a much needed shore leave where Kaushal would have to present his case.

Rezo hated to leave Tristan's fate unresolved. He also had his own ideas about Plan C, but he found Kaushal stubborn. The young man thought in violent terms. Why not? His culture was a violent culture. Humans beheading other Humans was something from Earth's dark past, barbarous acts created by savage minds.

Rezo wasn't a student of history, always preferring to look toward the future, but he didn't know of any Human group as savage as the First Tribe's leaders. There were some nasty people in the galaxy, Human or otherwise, perhaps only the Rangers escaping a return to savagery on colony worlds, but no world in ITUIP had a history like Eden's.

The planet's history wouldn't sway ITUIP's General Council. It could work against Kaushal. In spite of his stubbornness, the young man would need a more convincing plan. Rezo would try to guide him on that, but the captain knew he would need help. He was a dilettante in the intersentient politics present on major ITUIP planets.

Rezo's place was in space. He knew how to handle an ITUIP explorer ship. He could even steer the young prince in the wrong direction when he had to confront planetary VIPs. But he had an idea about who could help in finding the right direction.

Chapter Eighteen

New Haven

By the time the *Zheng He* arrived at New Haven, an E-type planet in the 82 Eridani system, Kaushal had learned his way around the ship. He had also met and chatted with some Rangers.

New Haven was also a watery world like Eden. From space, Kaushal spotted the largest islands and many archipelagoes. Many islands had no Human population , only Rangers, who had first colonized the planet long ago after their home world was invaded by the Talis, who had killed millions of Rangers there.

That history gave Kaushal pause. Earth had suffered a similar fate at the hands of Tali invaders, although not all Humans there were killed. *If Talis could change and become civilized members of ITUIP society, can the First Tribe? Or, is that beyond hope for certain groups of Humans?*

He'd discovered Lala had the same religion as Tristan. She was a Guide to the Way like Yago. Kaushal was able to continue his religious education under her, if it could be called that—it was more mystic philosophy than religion. In a few months, he had matured under her tutelage. It wasn't easy because he was attracted to her. And she didn't help by mixing flirting with serious philosophy. But he managed to control his emotions. He was beginning to understand many things, including people's needs and actions. But he was still stubborn about one thing: He couldn't imagine the First Tribe's leaders ever changing. They were too addicted to their evil ways.

And he would never forgive them for what they had done to his family, especially the First Pilgrim. If ITUIP wouldn't help, he would return to Eden and avenge all who had perished under the brutal yoke of the First Pilgrim.

For now, though, he would hide those thoughts and go along with Rezo.

***

At the spaceport, Kaushal saw many more non-Human genotypes than those appearing in the frescoes. Rangers outnumbered Humans and Humans outnumbered Tali. Rezo accompanied him, so he asked the captain to name other strange sentients he saw. There were so many he knew he couldn't remember all the genotypes, though, or where they were from.

"Look over there," said Rezo. "You can see the skyline of First Landing, where Humans founded their first colony."

"Why are buildings so high?"

"Land is at a premium like on Eden." They watched a small aircraft disappear into the forest of buildings. "High in the air, and far below ground, they go, with flitters commuting among buildings and trains crawling in the island's guts. It's a bit claustrophobic for me, even in a flitter, because buildings are all around you. Right over there, though, you can see the green patchwork of havenberry fields. Everyone works together to keep the planet healthy. Humans came here to pristine conditions, and they're still much the same—except for cities, of course, but even they have many parks at different levels."

"It looks busy," said Kaushal, spotting a half dozen more aircraft.

"Not so much at the level we're looking at, but below ground it's a zoo. Like I said, claustrophobic. New Haven is a busy place right now because it's their turn to be capital of ITUIP. That's rotated every ten standard years."

"Do all ITUIP worlds participate in the rotation?"

"So far, only the first Human colonies—New Haven, Sanctuary, and Novo Mondo. The Tali and Usk home worlds have petitioned to take part in the rotation. It will occur, but old resentments die slowly. We'd like to have a Swarm world or two in there too, but the Swarm is continuing to play coy. There's also some popular support for Earth, but the population is so low there, it isn't yet justified."

Kaushal had learned the history of Swarm, a collection of solar systems in a globular cluster whose inhabitants had become a single intelligence. It had played an important role in the history of ITUIP. The Union had a rich and varied history making Eden's seem small and insignificant.

"Earth is our home world, right?"

"Far in the past, but the First and Second Tribes originated on a planet named Demeter at the edge of ITUIP space, if that's what you're asking."

"Maybe that's what we call the Founder's Planet," said Kaushal. "I should study all this history before I make my presentation to ITUIP's General Council."

"You'll have time."

"Do you need a ride?" A robotaxi had pulled alongside them, bringing their attention back to ground level.

"There's no driver," said Kaushal with a smile.

"It's safer this way. And some taxis are specialized. For example, for Rangers, special seats are needed, and Talis need a bit of extra headroom. And many have flying capability like this one. Get in."

Kaushal became nervous as the robotaxi carried them into a stream of traffic and then took flight.

"New Haven is still considered agrarian," said Rezo, "which is another reason they keep cities from spreading. The biggest exports are havenberries and havenberry wine, but there also are a lot of dairy farms. New Haven exports cheese too. You'll feel right at home."

The taxi banked. Kaushal grabbed at a strap; Rezo leaned into the turn.

"We'll bunk in a hotel near the center of First Landing. I don't recognize the center anymore. It always changes between my visits. I spend most of my time in space."

"Monitoring us?"

"You already know we take turns at that. It's a mission lasting one standard year. Exploratory ships scout around for habitable planets and study their potential for colonies. Most go into a database. Your planets Paradise and Eden were two of them, but the First and Second Tribes colonized without permission from ITUIP. Didn't tell them. That often happens. It's why we have a lot of backward planets run by crazy fanatics."

"You consider us fanatics?"

"Not everyone, of course, but enough violent, murderous fanatics to worry us. ITUIP members are beyond that, so we like to watch you and make sure you behave and stay put where you are."

"Like we're diseased?"

"If you like, call it a quarantine." Rezo smiled. "We do. The ITUIP Protocol allows us to quarantine and monitor, not to interfere. Self-determination is desired. In other words, ITUIP wants a planet like yours to come to its senses and contribute to the advancement of civilization in this galactic neighborhood."

Kaushal nodded. "It sounds like obtaining an exception to the Protocol won't be easy. Are you going to help me?"

"Officially? No. That's on your shoulders. I'll give some advice until we have to return to space, as I've been doing. I'll try to find some good people who can serve as advisers for you in the interim and after we leave for our next mission."

"Has anyone been successful at obtaining an exception to the Protocol before?"

"No. But there always has to be a first time, right?"

***

The First Landing Hilton was in the city's old center, an unusual mixture of glitzy new structures and old buildings of historical importance. Rezo explained some of the historical sites after the robotaxi landed and became enmeshed in heavy road traffic.

"Were you born here?" said Kaushal.

"No. I was born on Hard Fist, outside ITUIP then, an ITUIP member planet now. My parents moved to Novo Mondo when I was young. I have one sister who returned to Hard Fist. The rest of my family still lives on Novo Mondo."

"Why did Humans pick these star systems for their first three colonies?"

"Who knows? Ancient history. I know 82 Eridani is a star similar to Earth's. Other first colonies, Sanctuary and Novo Mondo, also orbit suns like Earth's. Maybe that was a factor. I heard or read somewhere they'd discovered many worlds going around many stars by the time Humans left their home system, so maybe I'm wrong. You can learn about that if you want. Ask your implant."

Kaushal tapped the device at the side of his head. "I'm still getting used to it. I tend to ask in too general a manner, so I'm swamped with information."

"It takes a bit of practice. You have to zero in on what you want." The taxi came to a halt. "Here we are."

The robotaxi pulled into a semicircular drive covered by huge shade trees, but these were dwarfed by the building, its top floors disappearing into the clouds. "I hope you enjoyed your trip," said the taxi. "A robocart will take your luggage. Thank you for riding with First Landing Specialty Limo."

"We don't have luggage," said Rezo. He smiled at Kaushal. "Stupid machines. We can't live with them, and we can't live without them either. Some of them were made on Earth, one of their major industries now."

"Is it true Humans were once at war with Talis?"

"Rangers too. Because of that, Swarm wanted to destroy the Talis. We convinced it not to do it. Good thing, too. They contribute a lot to ITUIP now."

"Like Hamil?"

"Hamil's a first class ship's doc and one of my best friends. He interned with Carlos Obregon, an independent thinker who was the greatest ship's medical officer in recent history. I could have never been his captain, though. Independent thinker is putting it mildly. He was always getting into trouble. Everything usually turned out OK, but he gave his captain a hard time."

Kaushal smiled as Rezo waved his hand to open the sliding doors. "I can do that now without your help."

"Only for show on my part. You're considered a visiting dignitary. Live with it."

They went inside the cool interior of the hotel.

Chapter Nineteen

Planning the Petition

"We need to briefly mention your family's history," said Mera Deeson, a dark-haired woman who was a partner in a First Landing law firm. "That will achieve some sympathy."

Freson, a Tali nodded, and Skims-the-Waves, a Ranger buzzed his agreement. The local AI translated it all. Although Kaushal's dialect was derived from Human Standard, he had trouble with the latter, and he could catch only a few words of Tali and nothing of the Ranger's symbolic idiom. He wondered what would happen to this society if AIs started failing.

Deeson's skin was a beautiful ebony. Her lips seemed to be in a permanent pout even when she smiled, and her curly hair was in disarray. Freson was only a bit different from Hamil, Rezo's medical officer. Powerful muscles bulged under orange fur. His ears were constantly twitching. Skims-the-Waves reminded Kaushal of a huge version of the carnivorous bugs skimming across quiet water on Eden, except he had fur too and seemed to be the comedian in the trio. Their presence made Kaushal once again realize how wonderfully diverse life in the galaxy was, although he was only sampling some of it.

They were in a conference room at Deeson's firm. Modern furnishings didn't change its function; they were used like the stark rooms designed for the same function in Starlight Castle

"I don't want sympathy. I want the Council to recognize our cause is just." Kaushal studied Rezo. "I thought you said these people could help me?"

Rezo smiled at Deeson. "Patience isn't one of Kaushal's virtues, Mera."

"Considering his history, he's been patient," said Freson. He turned to Kaushal. His words were sympathetic; his leathery, black face was unreadable. Fortunately Kaushal had met Hamil. Talis were imposing fellows. "We can help you present your case to the Council. They're not eleven old idiots, Kaushal. They're smart people and listen carefully to a reasoned appeal. That's all they do, each one for ten years. They're the last recourse for ITUIP citizens and institutions. You've jumped over many lower councils due to your unique situation."

"We're a loose trade union," said Skims-the-Waves, "more separate than united most of the time. Originally we had trouble with that, but now that we understand our friends here—" he waved some tentacles at Deeson and Freson, "—it's natural. Maybe not for you yet, though. You see, each member planet has its own local government. Most of them are similar to New Haven's."

"Interplanetary Trade Union of Independent Planets," said Kaushal. "But Captain Rezo works for ITUIP."

"Member planets have to sign onto the idea that certain things like exploration and defense should be interplanetary yet still centralized," said Mera. "But don't think this Council will tell Rezo to invade Eden with guns blazing. That would set a bad precedent."

"And allow a bad metaphor," said Rezo with a growl and sending a scowl Deeson's way. "We have to be a bit more subtle. Guns, my ass!"

"How do we do that?" said Kaushal, disappointment in his voice.

"Our job is to create a plan," said Freson. "Where are you going, Rezo?"

"I received a message from an old friend who wants to meet for dinner. She's a lot prettier than Kaushal, and I haven't seen her for a while." He winked at Kaushal. "You're in good hands, lad. These three are the best, believe me. They'll help you create a good strategy."

Kaushal was uncomfortable watching Rezo leave. He had just met these people.

***

Julie Chen, ship's medic from the *Vasco da Gama*, was also on shore leave. After greetings and hugs, Rezo gave her a summary of the Eden situation.

Julie and Rezo were old friends. One of the famous Carlos Obregon's interns, she had forsaken a promising career in medical research to become a ship's medical officer. She and Obregon had been an exceptional team in the exploratory fleet, but the old rascal had insisted it was time for her to go her own way.

It had been a hard adjustment for her, but now she was maybe better than her mentor—at least for medical expertise. She could attend to almost every sentient genotype in ITUIP and also to many outside the Union. She also had special skills that had led to papers in electronic journals, and online videos of complicated surgeries she had performed, all studied in ITUIP's medical schools.

"They'll never go for it," she said, referring to Kaushal's quest. "It's too dangerous. No one wants fanatics like that overrunning near space. It's better to keep them isolated." *Although Obregon often ignored the Protocol!*

"I hear you. We were doing so. This Kaushal upset things a bit, although Tristan's deeply involved—the wily old fox is meddling too much." He smiled. "You're right. I see our strategy having various levels. Edenites have to become peaceful during a few standard decades at least. But the Council could decide to intervene to start that process because the situation is so bad. With continued monitoring and their good behavior, the Council's opinion about lifting the quarantine might soon change."

Julie nodded. Eden's case was somewhat similar to cases she had lived through as an intern on starship *Brendan*. Trouble often had found Carlos Obregon, and that trouble often involved her as well. With teeming billions in the Galaxy's near-Earth neighborhoods, trouble was nearly a statistical certainty. Most of the time it didn't happen on ITUIP planets, though.

"Even in the best cases, lifting quarantines has often taken many decades, even centuries. And the worlds involved weren't nearly so dangerous and fanatical. What do you want to do? Eradicate all the religious fanatics? You say these Wilders still believe in the Founder, his laws, and his prophecies. That's not a good start because that's crazy thinking. Such credos don't allow much room for progress."

"Deeson has the idea it can be as simple as increasing trade while maintaining the quarantine."

"That's been done before, sometimes successfully, but it puts a lot of high tech equipment in the hands of savages. That's always a danger."

It was Rezo's turn to nod. They both knew about the case of Adeline's World where non-Human crazies decided to destroy their planet and enter their version of heaven all at once, for example. They called it the Rapturous Voyage to Ultimate Perfection. They killed all ITUIP representatives and set off nuclear weapons planet-wide, committing mass suicide and turning their planet into a radioactive wasteland. Of course, that was nothing compared to Swarm, who had wanted to destroy the entire Tali Empire spread across multiple star systems.

Skirmishes on Eden were like child's play in comparison to the two cases, but she knew ITUIP's General Council always worried about risks—local problems often became more generalized. That biased their decisions toward conservatively maintaining the status quo.

"Where are you staying?" said Rezo after the robowaiter took their order.

She smiled. "You have Diana now. Does she know you're here?"

"Of course. You're still desirable and seductive, you know, but I'm just curious. Maybe you'd like to attend the Council hearing."

She sighed. "Possibly. I have a surgery to perform—there might be complications."

"But you're on shore leave too."

"The surgery is a favor for a crewmember. One of his relatives here on New Haven needs some special TLC."

"Human?"

"Ranger. The relative is from his home clan. I'm sure they could do the surgery, but I invented the technique about eighty standard years ago and can do it in my sleep. A victim of my own success, as they say. The poor relative has been limited to buzzspeak all her life."

Rezo nodded. For a Human, that was like being blind in one eye and short-sighted in the other. Rangers had two languages, the standard buzzspeak all AIs could translate, and a special underwater language for describing images and other underwater cues as well as transmitting lots more information, a language so complicated AIs couldn't handle it.

"I guess duty calls then," he said.

"But call me tomorrow. If all goes well with the surgery, I'd love to attend. I'm interested in seeing this Prince Kaushal in action."

Chapter Twenty

The ITUIP General Council

"All rise!" said the roboclerk.

Kaushal stood and watched the Council's members file in. There were special seats for each one—Rangers, Talis, and Humans. Other non-Humans were present in the Council chamber's audience. Curious onlookers, reporters and photographers were among the crowd too.

Only four members of the Council were Human. Kaushal had learned one Council member retired every year and another was asked to take her or his place. Terms lasted for ten years. *Some of them must have received short straws when this all started,* he thought, considering how practical such a setup would be on Eden.

He glanced at his three advisers who sat beside him.

"Relax," said Deeson in a whisper. "They're only people like us."

"I know that," he said, "but this is important for my planet and for me personally."

"Whatever happens here, you can return to Eden. She's still there."

"You know about Anju?"

Deeson nodded. "Through Tristan. He's reported in, by the way."

Kaushal smiled. "I knew he'd be OK. He's a survivor. Were any other names mentioned in his report?"

"Collectively. All your friends survived. Someone named Ezan was blinded in one eye, though, and someone named Kifi is still recovering from her wounds. Your people had many casualties."

"That's why I'm here. The killing must stop."

"In the case of Prince Kaushal of Eden versus ITUIP, will the plaintiff please step forward," said the roboclerk. Kaushal looked at Deeson; she nodded. Kaushal stepped toward the arc formed by the seated Council members. "Council is convened to hear a petition for removal of a quarantine on the planet Eden." There followed a long list of descriptors locating the planet within the galaxy but outside ITUIP and providing access numbers to files available to the public through their implants, files describing the planet's detailed history and reasons for quarantine. "Plaintiff may proceed."

"I'm here to plead the case for the people of Eden," he began. His team had coached him on what to say. Plan C consisted of ending bloodshed on Eden, appealing to compassion and respect for all sentient life, and continued monitoring and maintaining peace.

"I understand you represent only one side of the conflict," said a Ranger on the Council. "Does the other side have a representative here?"

Deeson stood. "The other side in this conflict wants nothing to do with anything going on in the galaxy outside Eden. They have created a brutal theocracy that exploits and murders all who would oppose it."

"You have provided ample evidence for this," said a Tali, "much of it collected using ITUIP surveillance, but if no spokesperson is present for the other side in the conflict to defend their point of view, how can we start these proceedings?"

"Can the plaintiff present a bit of his personal history?" said Deeson.

The Council debated but then agreed to hear that as long as it didn't take too long. Deeson nodded to Kaushal. He summarized how he had survived and came to be in this situation.

"Let me confirm," said the Tali. "Your people lost this recent battle for Eden?"

"The First Tribe's oppression will be worse now," said Kaushal after nodding. "Everyone in the Mountain Folk or Wilders caught by the First Tribe will now be tortured and beheaded."

"So your appeal reduces to getting us involved in a planetary civil war where ITUIP has no stake in the outcome," said one Human.

"And risk polluting the Galaxy with religious thugs," said the Tali.

"I'm sympathetic to your case," said the Ranger, "but we've been burned by these interventions before. That's the reason for the quarantine and monitoring program. People must resolve their own differences. It's an important Protocol. We're proud to have invented it. Its genesis occurred with Swarm."

"So you won't help us?" said Kaushal.

"We'll debate the case later in private sessions," said the Human. "We have two others on the docket today. For now, we're done with this one."

"How long will your decision take?"

"As long as we need. We'll be in touch."

***

"It doesn't look promising," Kaushal told Rezo back at their hotel. The captain from *Zheng He* had attended the session with Julie Chen, who now had an interest in the case.

"I've always been pessimistic," said Rezo, "but Deeson's team and you presented a good case to the Council. What will you do if they vote against your petition?"

"What would you do?"

"I'd try to steal your beautiful princess away from that hellhole and ask for asylum on some ITUIP planet, knowing I'd done my best."

"That's the safe route for us, I guess, but it won't help Eden's people. Yes, I'm inclined to return for Anju, no matter what, but if the Council offers no support, I'll also return to fight."

"I was afraid you'd say that. Maybe they shouldn't have told you Tristan and the others survived. Great Way, lad, you have to realize you'll most likely be returning to die. I can't recommend that as a smart choice for Anju or you."

"People here live long lives," said Kaushal, "so life becomes more precious to them. Rangers are naturally long-lived, but the rest, with their perfectly engineered bodies, excellent medical care, and longevity drugs, live for hundreds of standard years too. I suppose that's why Tristan has been around so long to help us—he's less risk-averse than you people. But for others on Eden, life is a struggle and lives are short. I'd prefer to die sooner in a noble cause than decades later of old age."

Rezo nodded. "I see your point, but you can go through a body scan here, eliminate any unwanted health problems, and then go on the drugs. Genetic engineering doesn't tamper with too much. Otherwise, we'd all look alike."

"If I did that and Anju didn't, I'd watch her grow old and die, along with all my friends on Eden, with the exception of Tristan."

"OK, we're getting off track here," said Rezo. "If the Council votes against your petition completely, how will you return to Eden?"

"You mean, not even allowing an increase in trade? Does that mean I'm stranded here?"

"Until the next changing of the watch for ITUIP monitors, that's for sure. After our leave, *Zheng He* will be off on other assignments. The larger ship that just replaced us will be there for a while because recent hostilities imply a longer and more detailed monitoring, perhaps with some boots on the ground to obtain detailed intel. I doubt you'll have that much patience."

"I'll have to find some other way."

"I don't recommend that, but, whatever you do, don't tell me about it. Your plans will be safer that way."

Kaushal smiled. "That makes sense. You'd have to tell them if they asked, right?"

"If I wanted to keep my job. Sometimes I wonder about that. There are cases like yours where I'm depressed by outcomes."

***

The petition was denied three standard weeks later. Deeson and her team invited Kaushal to drinks to help him drown his bitterness. When she left him at his hotel, she knew he would awake the next morning with a havenberry hangover. She did too. She figured it was worth it if they made the young prince a bit happier.

She still went early to check on him. She was afraid wine had only dulled his depression. With all their advanced medical techniques, mental depression still occurred and was still often treated with drugs. She was going to suggest that to Kaushal. She thought he might be suicidal. That wouldn't be a good ending to his adventures on New Haven.

But he was gone.

She called New Haven Security. They informed her they already had reports of a feral Human wreaking havoc among the population, cop-speak on New Haven for stolen money, IDs, and food, all rare occurrences. Incidents were random enough she knew Kaushal didn't have many ideas about where to go or what to do. That put him in danger from both the official and illegal sides.

She explained the case to the people she talked to; they promised to handle Kaushal gently even if he became violent. She'd have to let Security handle it. They were the pros.

She subvocalized to close the comlink with her implant—incidents occurred even in the tame society of New Haven. Kaushal would be arrested; she didn't want anything more than that to happen. *May he use the Way to find peace.*

Part Four

The Return

The speediest way to communicate in known space is still via starship. Swarm made sure of that when it closed off other pathways through the multiverses. That's too bad. I'd like to communicate more with my grandchildren.

—Carlos Obregon, medical officer (ret) of starship *Brendan*

Chapter Twenty-One

Planet Hopping

The Tali captain studied the disheveled Kaushal. *Is he wondering about my sanity?* Rezo had told him low-level crewmembers on a merchant ship didn't have quality lives. They were often escaping some situation too, and the stress of cramped quarters and wondering how to better their lives often led to skirmishes that could turn deadly.

"We'll need a police clearance," said Captain Kulboi. "I have to comply with New Haven laws here and ITUIP laws in general. I need to be able to prove you're not wanted by Security. That's the way it is."

Kaushal looked around and bent low, forgetting that no matter how softly he spoke, the Tali would hear him through his com implant. "What if you pay me half what you pay others?"

Kulboi's fuzzy ears twitched, a sign of attention. Via body language, Kaushal knew he was making progress.

"That wouldn't add much to my share at journey's end, and I would still run the risk of incurring authorities' wrath. We don't have good reputations to start with. They all assume we smuggle stolen goods, for example."

"OK, what if I work for free? Food and air will be my pay. And a ride to your next stop. How can you pass up a deal like that?"

"Look, I'm not signing you on unless you tell me your story. It's hard enough being the captain of this tub without having New Haven Security on my back. I've worked hard to keep my name clean, which is more than I can say for some of my crew. Make your story good so I'll at least be sympathetic."

"OK. Can I sit?"

Kulboi nodded. Kaushal sat and began his tale of woe. When he finished, the twitching of Kulboi's ears had become a blur.

"By my ancestors, I could never create a tall story like that. Is this all true? Can I confirm it?"

"The Council's proceedings are public record. You can access that now with your implant. I need to return to Eden, no matter how long it takes. Your ship would be but a first leg in that journey, I'm sure."

"How will you run the blockade imposed by ITUIP's monitoring ship?" said Kulboi. "Assuming you can return to Eden, of course."

Kaushal shrugged. "I'm making it up as I go."

"I guess you'll have time to worry about the end game. You'll be planet hopping for a while. Maybe many years."

***

Kaushal's problem? There was no trade with Eden anymore, via ITUIP or otherwise. No one dared violate ITUIP's quarantine. The ITUIP ship in orbit around the planet was only of average size in the large fleet of exploratory starships, but it was still well armed compared to any merchant ship. This ship had two missions: keep the planetary population confined to the planet, and keep others from off-planet from landing. It was an embargo as well as a quarantine. While some non-ITUIP ships had managed to land either because they carried essential supplies or they used the planet as a screen, most no longer bothered—the last ship had landed years ago.

But it didn't take Kaushal years to come near Eden. He arrived on Quick Death fourteen standard months later, a planet only eleven light years from his home. He found work in a mine to make some money and began to plan how he would complete the final leg of his journey. He knew it might be the most difficult. The ITUIP ship replacing *Zheng He* was larger than Captain Rezo's ship with more arms and more security personnel. Even getting to Eden's solar system would be difficult.

He met Kiana at a local bar. She was studying him when he turned to survey the few customers present. He smiled at her but returned to his drink. Unlike other miners in the pub, he wasn't looking for sex.

He wanted to be alone with his thoughts. The pounding music—he assumed it was Human in origin, but he didn't recognize it—made that difficult. It was heavy on the bass, shaking the bar, clinking stored glasses, and making waves in his drink at times. They had an old saying on Eden that described the situation well: he couldn't hear himself think. And there was no reason to have it that loud unless most patrons were deaf—the music came from an old sound system working independently of the planetary AI, so they only had to turn it down. He decided not to ask. The patrons didn't look too friendly.

That brief glance had told him she was a bit exotic. Short black hair framed a face with high cheekbones and thin lips. Her epicanthic folds reminded him of Tristan. She had been tapping her finger on the table. *Wondering whether to approach me?* He was betting it would cost a month's salary to bed her, but he had to smile at the thought. Anju seemed far away, even if it was only eleven lightyears.

"You look like you need some company, stranger," she said to his back.

The pitch of her voice floated above the pub's strident music. A nice voice, but with some power to it. And she had spoken to him in his own dialect. *Can it be? Is she from Eden?*

He studied her in the mirror behind the roboserver. She stood and approached him. She was tall but well proportioned. Her smile was enigmatic as if she enjoyed some private joke. An older woman. *Is she selling her body?* Mining camps were filled with such women, but she was a cut above the norm. She took the stool next to his.

"Don't give me the line, 'what's a nice girl like you doing in a place like this?'" she said. "I'm not a—" the old AI his implant was connected to couldn't translate the local word, but he understood the meaning. "I work in the mining office. You clean up well, by the way. I've seen you coming from the tunnels. Pretty bad down there, isn't it?"

He shrugged. "It's a job. I'm not complaining. What do you do in the office?"

"Accounting. Data entry, calculating profit and loss— things like that. I'm trying to make enough money to leave here."

"You were born here, I take it." *So, how do you know my dialect?*

"Believe it or not, in the north there's farmland. It's mostly deserted now. Most farmers found it more profitable to work in the mines. I'd still like to return, buy my folks' old farm, and have a bunch of kids in a safe place where men don't look at you like a slab of meat."

"Not too many Human females around for all the Human males," said Kaushal. "And I'm not looking at you like a slab of meat. You remind me of a friend." He was now thinking of Kifi instead of Tristan. "More personality than looks, though. Why single me out? I must be ten years younger and not the best husband material. I'm moving on as soon as I determine how to do it."

"My implant tells me you're from Eden. Where's that and what's it like?"

He realized she was now speaking Standard and the AI was translating for him. *Did I imagine she spoke to me in my dialect?* He stared at his drink. *I must be getting drunk!*

"In some ways, it's nicer than here. In others, this is far better. But I'm trying to return, no matter what opinion is correct."

He could see her throat moving. *Subvocalization query to her implant.*

"It's under ITUIP quarantine. That often goes both ways. How did you ever leave there?"

"That's a long story. Let's find more comfortable chairs and a table where I can buy you a drink and tell you all about it." *Yes, I must be drunk. She's a complete stranger. Drink and the stirring in my loins will make a fool of me.*

Chapter Twenty-Two

Another Love

Days passed quickly after meeting Kiana. Her openness and love for life reminded Kaushal of Anju, Kifi, and Ezan. At first he would feel guilty falling into her bed at night, but she was more than a casual lover: he could scheme with her about plans for returning to Eden.

"I want to see your home turf," he said to her one night, spooning after some passionate love-making.

She was skilled in helping him shake off weariness from the work in the mines, and, in the process, shake off hers too. She worked ten-standard-hour shifts at her job— the bosses were stern and demanding taskmasters. Hers was mental fatigue, his physical.

"We don't have any time off," she said. "I have two jobs because they need me to resuscitate their damned AI all the time. It's most likely a few hundred-years-old. It even has a name."

"I didn't know AIs had names. What's the name of yours?"

"Ours. Your implant is serviced by it too. The name's Grim Reaper. Grim Reaper in the service of Quick Death. Understand? Some asshole had a strange sense of humor. Maybe while on his death bed dying from lung disease acquired from breathing dust from heavy metal ores? Medical services here are primitive. Longevity is a meaningless word for a miner unless he finds a way to leave this rock."

"Humor's hard to find on this planet, so I'll take strange. But the only time I smile is making love with you."

"We can't become too close, Kaushal," said Kiana. "We'll eventually need to go our separate ways, most likely you before me. We're having a good time, but it has to end. You do realize that, right?"

"I don't see how I can go anywhere." He patted her head. "That's why I wanted to see your old farm. Captain Rezo Banton back on New Haven told me to settle somewhere and forget about Eden. I can do that and be part of your life and maybe forget with time."

"Oh, please, you're no farmer. And what about your Anju?"

"They might have forced her to marry the new king by now."

"You can still kill that king and carry her off. Or, don't you love her anymore? That would prove my point, by the way: you're young and immature. You confuse making love with being in love."

Kaushal turned red. "Of course I love her. I always will. But maybe I can never be with her. ITUIP won't let me. Here I escaped from hell, yet I'm still a prisoner. You're my one way past this impasse."

"And you'd settle for me? That makes me feel like a spare part for an old flitter."

He thought a bit. "Kings and princes can have harems on Eden. My father had several wives. Maybe it's a biological mutation, something in our genes."

"Several wives? That sounds impractical. Women can do it forever, but men only have so much stamina. And, in any case, one partner at a time is enough. The plumbing sort of dictates it."

Now Kaushal thought of Kifi and Ezan and smiled. "There are ways. Besides, it's not all about sex, you know. There's more than lust involved."

She smiled. "No, it's not all about sex." She turned toward him and kissed him. "But I'd like to know what's going on in your mind when you're inside me. Are you thinking about me, Anju, or some imaginary paradise where you have dozens of sexy females at your beck and call? Let's talk about it, and maybe we can do it again, Prince Kaushal."

Afterwards, while he listened to her soft snores, he was awake for hours wondering about their future. *Am I genealogically programmed to establish a harem?* It was an interesting idea. If so, Anju, Kifi, Ezan, and Kiana represented a good start. His last thought before sleeping was that outcome would be silly and egotistical and maybe asking for a lot of trouble. Maybe Kiana was right. Harems were biologically impractical. And maybe each woman should have multiple husbands instead. Miners on Quick Death would certainly go for that plan....

Chapter Twenty-Three

A Wanted Human

Weeks later, Kaushal stared into Kiana's tired eyes and brushed back her raven hair while looking for words. She smiled at him, possibly expecting the passionate kiss leading to a second round of lovemaking and then sleep. He was on his way there but paused.

"You're a bit distant tonight," she said.

"Frustrated is more like it."

"I told you women have more stamina than men. And men never listen. Let's go to sleep. I'm willing, but you're too tired."

He smiled. "Yes, that's an immediate frustration, but not the principal one. I don't see any solution to my problem of returning to Eden. It all reduces to needing a starship that will take me there, but no merchant ships visit the planet— only ITUIP monitors."

She propped herself on an elbow. "They don't come here much either. We might as well have a quarantine too." She smiled again, this time her eyes bright with mischief. "Why don't we steal one?"

"A ship? I don't know how to fly a starship."

"I do, in a way. Always wanted to, so I've taken courses and practiced with simulators. With the ship's AI, there isn't much to it. The captain is present more to keep crewmembers in line when they're on or near a planet, and crewmembers are there for in-flight maintenance and to take care of cargo and passengers, if there are any. The AI takes care of most flight details and is indispensable. No living organism has the mental capacity or speed of thought to navigate through multiverses."

"I'm guessing there's a big difference between a simulator and the real thing," said Kaushal. "Am I wrong?"

"Wrong or right, what do you have to lose? You said you can't find another solution. I'm offering you one." Her mischievous eyes were still sparkling.

"Assuming we can steal a ship and escape Quick Death, how do we run the blockade around Eden?"

"You tell them who you are," she said. "Why would they shoot at Eden's prince?"

"Because the First Pilgrim wants them to do that? Or because ITUIP wants to enforce the quarantine?"

"I'm pretty sure the ITUIP crew doesn't care much about what the First Pilgrim wants. And let's worry about them enforcing the quarantine when we arrive there. Right now we need to determine which ships are here and waiting for us to steal them."

***

"I have this strange feeling you've done this before," said Kaushal in a whisper. He slapped at some local bugs, receiving her shushing finger again. "Maybe you were a professional thief?"

The two were hidden behind shipping crates at the edge of Quick Death's tiny spaceport. Their bodies cast double shadows. One moon was a quarter full, the other half, but they were rarely new together, so Quick Death's nights were almost always moonlit.

It wouldn't have been smart to be there in the company's white overalls, so they dressed in black clothing, wore black berets, and Kiana had rubbed black soot over their faces. They looked like shadows too, even in the moonlight.

"I'll ignore that question. Isn't she a beaut?"

Kaushal studied the ship parked on the tarmac. Kiana called it a rich man's yacht. After Rezo's ship, this one appeared tiny and ready to be junked. It was smaller than Tristan's ship that had carried him to the ITUIP ship in orbit. He knew they'd only have one chance to make their escape. *Even if we're up to the task, is the ship?*

"What's it called again?"

"*Mosca.* I think that's a name for an ancient Earth insect. I looked up the plans. It's cozy inside, but we'll be comfortable. Mining execs use it to scout for other mining possibilities in this hellish solar system. But it has the full superstring drive. That hasn't changed much in thousands of years. Physics doesn't change."

"I'm not sure what that means, so I'll take your word for it. But maybe the ship is that old? It doesn't look safe. And how do we get inside?"

"I'll need some time to figure that out, but I'm good at making and breaking security codes. It shouldn't be difficult to get access. They're lax about security here. What miner would steal a starship?"

"This miner would," said Kaushal.

"I mean, what normal persons would? Most people wouldn't know that wreck has interstellar capability. I do, though, because of where I work. C'mon."

They were soon in shadows under the edge of the fuselage. The ship was ovoid and sat on six spindly legs as if it were a dormant insect, in line with the ship's name. Kaushal patted the lackluster hull.

"Lots of dents and pits," he said.

"It doesn't have to be aerodynamic. Landing and takeoff can be as slow as we want. This model even hovers.

At least that's what the damn manual says. I read the entire file."

"I'd make it rise as fast as possible in case we make some people mad at us for stealing it."

"There's that. Stay here." She climbed a short ladder and crouched by the entryway to study a keypad by the door. "I'm guessing four digits. Let's try 1-2-3-4."

That didn't work. She tried the corner numbers, first 1-3-7-9, and then other combinations. 1-3-9-7 worked. There was a hiss and the door slid open.

"Come aboard, my handsome lad, and let's fly this bucket of bolts," she said.

He hesitated as he peeked inside but then followed, deciding there was no recourse but to trust Kiana and her piloting ability.

***

"When Humans discovered FTL," she said to him from the pilot's chair, "theory came before practice, as it often does, so there were some weird accidents. People getting torn apart or turned inside out by strange topologies, AIs going wacko in strange multiverses, and so forth. Now it's all user friendly. I'd wager most pilots don't know the theory anymore. Ships come off the assembly line, and AIs do all the work. They have to; no biological sentient can handle it. The live crew is almost superfluous. Better said, they're needed for other things."

"Does this AI work independently of Grim Reaper?"

"Yes and no, but good question. It has to converse with Reaper for takeoff from Quick Death, but every ship needs its own AI. And they've been developed and improved a lot more than the basic FTL drive. There are technologies you can improve upon; others not so much."

"How do you know all this?"

"My courses, remember? I've dreamed of doing this for a long time. I'm leaving here, whether you come or not."

"I'm in the ship, aren't I?" He thought a moment. "But we're going to Eden. How can that work for you?"

"Anywhere but here, as they say. Maybe I'll have my farm on Eden. Nothing says I have to stay there, though. We'll hide the ship somewhere. I can leave whenever I want. I'd like to see your planet first, though."

"You could have done this by yourself without having to go to Eden."

She squeezed his knee and blew him a kiss. "I needed someone to motivate me. Hold on."

"Don't we have to file a flight plan and ask permission to takeoff?"

"Are you joking? Even if I knew who to ask, what am I going to say? I'm stealing starship *Mosca,* so please let me takeoff? I'm even cutting all communication with Quick Death, including Grim Reaper, as soon as possible. Maybe it will drive the ship's AI mad, but we don't have a choice."

He laughed. "I'm sufficiently ignorant that I don't know whether you're kidding me or not. I hope you are."

"Don't worry, my love. This will be easy. Believe me. Sit back and enjoy the ride."

It was easy. They soon left Quick Death's solar system. Kiana ordered the ship's AI to go FTL as soon as possible. After that, it took nearly five standard days to skip through the appropriate multiverses, but they reentered their own outside Eden's solar system.

"It might be tricky from here on," said Kiana. "I'm going to circle the star and ride with the solar wind until we go into orbit around Eden. That way it will be hard for their sensors to spot us, and the planet will be between us and ITUIP's monitoring ship when we're near. We'll then need to find an isolated landing spot where I can hide the ship and us from the natives. You can help with that."

"You don't need to hide from Mountain Folk or Wilders, only the First Tribe's cutthroats."

"I don't want anyone but us to know where the ship is. Things might have changed since you were here last. Let's not trust anyone too soon. We need to reconnoiter a bit."

A day later, they finally landed the ship in a high mountain meadow surrounded by ragged basaltic cliffs and not far from Dragon's Mountain.

"There's only one problem with your choice," said Kaushal, looking around, seeing pristine forest and a lake, but dismayed by the surrounding vertical terrain. "How do we climb out of here? Mountain Folk most likely are somewhere near, but we'll have to scale those cliffs."

"Maybe that gentleman will help us," said Kiana, pointing.

Kaushal shaded his eyes and peered into the sun. At the edge of a copse of trees, a figure was striding toward them. As he approached, Kaushal smiled. It was an old friend.

But Kiana beat him to Tristan. She jumped on him, wrapping her legs around his waist, and hugged him. He smiled and winked at Kaushal.

"It's been a while," said the Mountain Folk leader, "but I knew you'd be back."

"How'd you know we'd be here?" said Kaushal, grasping his hand after he lowered Kiana.

"Kiana told me," he said, nodding toward her.

"What? You know Kiana?" *A stupid question, of course!* "How?"

"It's a long story. Do you people have any food?"

"Only what's in our backpacks," said Kiana. "There's a stream running into the lake. I bet that water's cold and pure. I'm thirsty. I couldn't increase the humidity to the proper level on that bucket of bolts. It will become a good asset, though."

"For now that water will quench your thirst. But always ask me first. The First Pilgrim is starting a program of poisoning mountain lakes and streams. He hasn't reached this far yet, though, due to the terrain. Let's also have some nourishment. While we're doing that, I'll tell you the long story, Kaushal."

Chapter Twenty-Four

The Reunion

Kiana, Kaushal, and Tristan took ten days to hike through green valleys and high mountain passes, sometimes even through snow, until they found a Mountain Folk encampment. From a steep ledge they gazed down into the valley containing crude tents and lodges. Kaushal felt like he was home. He turned to his friend.

"Are Kifi and Ezan down there?"

"No, they're in another encampment, nearer Dragon's Head. We decided to have many smaller camps to make it harder for the king's Royal Guards to find us. They might destroy one of them, but others will survive."

Kiana elbowed Kaushal in the ribs. "I'm not enough for you, big boy?"

He smiled. "Probably more than enough, now that I know you're an ITUIP agent like Tristan. You sure fooled me, but for now, we'll forget about how manipulated I feel."

Kiana frowned and Tristan shrugged. "It was necessary," he said. "I thought you might be able to convince ITUIP authorities, although the likelihood was small and dependent on who's in the Council. It didn't occur, so we needed you back. A Plan C. We'll have to win Eden the hard way now."

"We already tried that," said Kaushal. "I'm surprised you weren't all killed. I feel guilty about deserting you. We lost a lot of valuable time by my petitioning the Council."

"You might have died too," said Kiana. "More so than ever before, the opposition to the First Pilgrim now needs a unifying leader. I don't see anyone else who fits the bill. Whether you like it or not, you're people's last hope."

Kaushal jerked a thumb at Tristan. "This fellow qualifies. Kifi and Ezan too. I've met others much more qualified than I am."

"But you bring everyone together," said Tristan. "You did that well before. People rallied behind you. We failed a bit by underestimating the foe, but we almost succeeded. We only need to sharpen our strategies."

"Maybe we should stay in the mountains and live our lives peacefully." He pointed to some figures below. "Those people don't have a care in the world. If the First Pilgrim leaves us alone, we can share Eden and wait for the First Tribe to come to its senses."

"I can understand how depressed you are," said Kiana. "And for many reasons."

"If we can stop debating historical mistakes, I have just the thing to cheer Kaushal up," said Tristan. "Let's stop talking and start moving."

It was a treacherous descent into the valley. Kaushal knew it would be more difficult coming back up. He couldn't have done it without Tristan guiding him. He enjoyed the thought that the First Pilgrim's soldiers would have a much more difficult time if they ever tried to mount an attack.

A few children tending to a small herd of jonkis ran to meet them. The biggest boy studied Kaushal. "Is he our new king?" he said to Tristan.

"Yes, I'm the king of the jonkis," said Kaushal, "or no one's king. I don't want to rule. But I've returned to help plan another campaign against the bad king and his Guards. Will that do for now?"

The boy nodded and offered his hand. Kaushal shook it. "I'll fight with you, Prince Kaushal. When we win, we'll make you king."

"Enough," said Tristan, tousling the boy's dark hair. "Where is everyone?"

"Being lazy," said a small girl who had joined the boy. "We had a big feast last night. The silly grown-ups were out of control. Hunters killed a shakma that had been eating our jonkis. We had fresh meat. His mate must be around somewhere, so it's us against her!" She brandished a small spear.

Tristan held up a hand. "Too much information. I guess we'll surprise those sleeping off their hangovers after they wake up." He pointed ahead. "Any traps on the way in?"

"Always," she said.

"Guide us then," he said.

***

The boy showed them the clever traps as they walked. Tripwires that would release heavy tree limbs with enough force to take a person's head off. Pits covered with light sticks, weeds, and grass, with sharpened stakes at the bottom tipped with poison. Mines that arose when stepped on, spraying shrapnel around a large circle. Poisoned dried meat and fruit hanging from tree limbs. Kaushal lost track of the different kinds of ingenious traps. He didn't remember these in his previous stay with Mountain Folk. The implications were clear: they were in a war-time defensive mode now.

"Are loyalist soldiers more present in the mountains?" he said to Tristan.

"They're on a mission to exterminate all of us," he said. "King Farben has become as bloodthirsty as Gol Kovlyn, the First Pilgrim, maybe more so. He's increased the Guard's size by fivefold and offered a sizable reward for every Mountain

Folk or Wilders' head. To pay for that, he's increased taxes, driving all his citizens farther into poverty."

"That's worse than I thought. They're bent on revenge."

"That's about the size of it. We hurt them a lot, even though they won, and they want to even the score. We've arrived."

Tristan fell into a lotus position in some green grass surrounding a primitive watering hole, a spring feeding a small creek that wound farther into the valley. Kiana joined him.

"Sit, Prince Kaushal," said the boy. "You've come a long way."

"Tristan promised me a surprise," said Kaushal, looking around.

"You'll be standing a while then," said Tristan. "I'm not going to disturb anyone's slumbers."

"Shouldn't there be sentries?" said Kaushal, joining the two and receiving a crude drinking goblet from the boy.

"Their eyes were watching you all the way," said the boy, filling the cup from a large earthen pitcher filled with cold water from the spring. "I'm training for that. We're taught to be invisible. We depend on more than traps, you see."

"Good plan," said Kaushal, trying the water. "So we wait for the silly grown-ups."

***

Kaushal was still dozing when the village awakened, starting with the young and ending with the elderly. Most greeted them and went about their business. Kaushal saw the faces of some old friends, but most of them were new to him.

"Kaushal?" said a voice behind him.

He knew that voice, jumped up, and turned. "Anju!"

"The surprise," said Tristan, with a smile.

Kaushal ran to hug her. Her timidity surprised him. "Is there something wrong?"

"I'm not to blame," she said. "There was nothing I could do. He raped me."

"Who? How?"

"Farben. Guards had to hold me down. I wanted to scratch his eyes out. I'm carrying his child."

"This is more than a surprise," Kaushal said to Tristan.

He shrugged. "She escaped and is with us now. But she's another reason Farben hunts us with such intensity. He wants his child. I'm not sure he wants the mother, though. We suspect she's in grave danger."

"He'll have to kill me to get him!" said Anju.

Kaushal sank to his knees in front of Anju. "We'll raise him as our own. I'll do anything to be with you. And never fear: Farben's days are numbered!"

"And your friend here? Who is she?" Anju flashed a smile at Kiana.

Kiana stood, approached Anju, and hugged her. "Don't worry, Kaushal owes me nothing. I betrayed him."

"Because you didn't tell me you knew Tristan and were ITUIP's agent?" said Kaushal, standing and grabbing her by the shoulders. "I don't consider that betrayal."

"I-tweep? Who's that?" said Anju.

Tristan joined them. "Let's keep certain things to ourselves for now, Kaushal. Remember what I said?"

He nodded. "OK. Kiana is just a dear friend, like Kifi and Ezan."

Anju nodded, picking up on some need for secrecy. "I suppose you're talking about people we saw from the electronic junk room." She smiled at Kiana. "If you brought

Kaushal back to me, you've helped him a lot more than I could. I hope to remedy that. I've met Kifi and Ezan, Kaushal. I don't mind. A great ruler can have many wives. I only want to be the first." She winked at Kiana and put a hand on Kaushal's cheek. "If you'll have me."

"Oh my, how pathetically romantic Humans can become," said Tristan, looking skyward. "Looks like we'll have to have another party in this encampment celebrating the prince's harem. Kiana's here, but should we wait for the return of Kifi and Ezan?"

"Can't I have some time alone with Kaushal first?" said Anju. "If Kiana's willing, that is."

"Sounds like a recipe for several parties," said Kiana, "but let's have a welcome home party first. We can discuss domestic life and battle strategies later."

"Maybe there's time for all that, but we need to move along the road to bringing peace and well-being to citizens of this beleaguered planet," said Tristan. "No discussion can change the fact we are all marked for death by the Royal Guards. These folks here might have had enough parties and now want to begin the business of saving this planet."

Kaushal winked at Tristan. His mentor smiled.

Part Five

The Golden Scimitar

We Humans have had our share of bad encounters with other galactic civilizations. It always amazes me, though, that Humans can create their own societies that can so brutalize other groups of Humans. It was enough to turn me away from the Way.

—Brent Mueller, ex-Guide to the Way and hero of Sanctuary

Chapter Twenty-Five

The Spies

"We need to enter Starlight Castle," said Kaushal.

Chobi, the pub's owner who had befriended Kaushal after he killed King Breman, looked from Kaushal to Anju and Tristan. He was a member of the opposition now. He was more jovial than before, though, a man with a higher purpose, it seemed. Tristan had explained that knowing they had company in the struggle to liberate Eden from the First Pilgrim's brutal theocracy made all the difference to many Edenites, especially to the downtrodden in Angels' Bay.

Chobi was still a large man but had slimmed a little, as much from honing his fighting skills as from food shortages often plaguing the capital under the First Tribe's rule. He poured another round of drinks from the large jug as they schemed in candlelight in the basement. Kaushal suggested an approach to the castle by sea.

"If you have a way in, we can get you near the seawalls," he said to Kaushal and Tristan.

"I won't be going," said Tristan, "only Kaushal and Anju. They know the castle better than I do. An old fishing boat will work best."

Kaushal nodded.

"That should be easy," said Chobi. "Good camouflage too. The water's deep there and the fishing good. There are always boats around. But how will you get inside?"

"I know ways," said Kaushal. "We'll need strong but light rope and a grappling hook."

"It seems dangerous," said Chobi. "It's like entering a hungry shakma's den."

Kaushal smiled. The elusive creatures were ferocious enough, but they became worse if they were trapped in a den with cubs inside to protect. The six-limbed creature had four paws with long claws and three-fingered clawed hands to grab its prey with. They were Eden's most ferocious predator. Even city folk respected their ferocity, although they often exaggerated it in drinking sessions.

"We know our way about the castle. We can hide there forever."

"But why is this so important?" said Chobi. "Why don't we plan another overall attack against the bastards?"

"That didn't work well before," said Tristan. "We need to demoralize the king and First Pilgrim's supporters."

"And we need to put them both into a rage," said Anju. "They'll make mistakes that way."

Chobi nodded. "I see. It's better not to tell me details. I'm under suspicion. Some informers told Royal Guards Kaushal went through this neighborhood. They figure someone helped him. They have long memories. After the battles, they've tortured people, trying to make them confess. I'm always looking over my shoulder. I also have my escape route planned."

"I need you on the boat," said Kaushal. "I trust you, old man."

"The fishermen on the boat will be trustworthy too, I assure you, but I'll be there, lad. I know those waters as well as they do. I used to smuggle contraband in from Wilders' boats right under their noses during dark nights." He winked at them. "I financed the purchase of this pub with some of the proceeds when I retired."

They clanked their tankards of ale and made detailed arrangements.

***

The tide was in, but it was so dark they could see only the waves' phosphorescent tips. Eden's four moons were either below the horizon or in the planet's shadow. Looking skyward, Kaushal thought he could see a bright pinpoint of light. *ITUIP monitors?* Did they know he'd returned? Had Tristan or Kiana informed them? *No matter. ITUIP has done little to help us, so to hell with them.*

Anju gripped Kaushal's hand.

"I hate this place," she said, looking toward the looming walls of the castle.

He understood the sentiment. The castle complex, Farben's abode and center for Eden's only religion, had become a symbol of evil.

"About there," came Chobi's whisper. "Get the hook ready, Jabon."

In the castle wall above, a person with sharp eyes could just make out a dark opening Kaushal knew well. The boat slowed, but they didn't drop anchor. There was a pfft! and the hook went skyward, dragging the rope behind it. They failed on the first try, but it caught on the second. Jabon, the sailor in charge of the air cannon used more for harpoons, pulled the rope taut.

"Now!" Kaushal said to Chobi.

Chobi wrapped his hirsute arms around Anju in a strong embrace.

"What's going on?" she said.

"It's too dangerous for you," said Kaushal.

She raised a knee into Chobi's groin and pushed the old man aside, managing to stand in the rocking boat with hands on hips to confront Kaushal. "Oh, no you don't! This is my battle too."

"We don't have time to argue," said Kaushal, feeling sorry for his old friend who was groaning with both hands on his family jewels.

"So, climb the rope already. I'll be right behind you, as planned. And don't ever exclude me again or you'll feel my knee too!"

He shrugged. He decided he had yet to learn never to underestimate headstrong women.

"Let's go then."

***

Kaushal helped Anju into the opening. They waved to Chobi and the boat's crew below.

"They should have put bars here," said Anju with a smile.

"They did. I removed them long ago. They were set in old mortar that had eroded from the salt air and seawater. In storms, waves can crash this high. That's why this tunnel slopes upward."

"What was it used for?"

"You can't see them, but there's a row of openings for cannons and snipers' rifles dating back to my father's time and before. The First Tribe doesn't know about this place."

"Where are we going?"

"The junk room first. Tristan made an equipment request. You can help me find what he needs."

"Thank you for asking me to contribute something. Did Tristan order you to keep me in the boat?"

"I arranged it with Chobi. I'd die if anything happened to you. And don't be mad. You contribute by being at my side."

"I'd appreciate it if you'd recognize I've developed some skills while staying with Mountain Folk."

He kissed her. "I recognize that. Chobi's balls will be aching for days. But I still don't want you in danger."

"Men! Always assuming we're the weaker sex. What about Kiana, Kifi, and Ezan? Do you treat them like helpless females too?"

"This isn't the time to debate women's rights," said Kaushal. "Let's head for the junk room."

"It's dark. How will we find our way?"

"Lights come on as we walk. Remember? Even here. The First Tribe only uses technology for evil. My father used it in better ways. And he often had fun with it."

Chapter Twenty-Six

Back in the Castle

Soon they entered the room filled with electronic rubble. Anju stared at the dark screens. "You have to tell me more about this ITUIP. What are those people doing up there?"

"It's a long story," said Kaushal, "but they're monitoring us. Our planet's quarantined. They can't interfere because of something called a Protocol."

"But Kiana and Tristan are their agents?"

"Some bend ITUIP's rules a bit. Not enough to satisfy me, though."

He remembered that his team had told him not to mention Tristan. Now he understood why. It was likely buried in gigabytes of records, but there would be a record of Tristan's descent to Eden in that ship. Kaushal was sure of that. He wondered if that would have changed the Council's decision. *Maybe make it worse?*

"Forget the screens. Here's Tristan's list."

It took the remainder of the day to sort through all the junk to find equipment and spare parts matching Tristan's request. They packed it all in two large cloth sacks.

"What now?" said Anju. "I'm tired."

He put his hand on her belly. "Another reason I didn't want you to come."

"It's the tyrant's," she said. "I don't care if I lose this baby, Kaushal. It's the Devil's spawn."

"He's part you, isn't he? That works in his favor. We can nurture the child to follow the Way, not this pathetic religion. So I care, especially if it means you die in childbirth. You are strong, but this won't be easy. We're a team, right?"

"Give it up, Kaushal. I know it won't be easy. But, if we die, we die together."

"OK." He kissed her again. "To answer your question, we rest until midnight and then we do a bit of stalking. Equipment isn't all I've come for."

"Are you going to clue me in?"

"Will you promise to rest with me?"

"Of course. I already said I was tired. What are you here for?"

"I'm going to steal the Golden Scimitar."

***

When they awoke from their short nap, they ate a light snack and prepared for their mission. Already dressed in black, they smeared charcoal-impregnated grease on their faces, and then made their way back into the castle.

"Will the First Pilgrim be in his chambers?"

"The Scimitar is in a wall safe in his study." Kaushal waved a bag of dried weeds. "But we'll have to go through his bedroom. This will do the trick."

He found the button. The wall panel slid open. They stepped into a dark room. He found a dish and put the bag's contents in it. He handed Anju a cloth wet with sea water and took one for himself.

"Why don't we kill him?" said Anju. "He deserves it."

Kaushal shrugged. "I suppose. I have something against killing a holy man in his sleep, though. Farben is different, after what he did to you. But he sleeps with prostitutes now. In a sense, they're his victims too, but they might wake him."

She nodded. "I wish one would cut his balls off. I'd like to torture him myself."

Kaushal studied her. It was the first time he had seen her so desirous of revenge. *My sweet Anju has been warped by that monster.* He shrugged again. He didn't have time to debate moral issues or vengeance, though.

"Cover your mouth and nose," he said, striking a match. The old man in the bed stirred but was soon snoring again as acrid smoke filled the room. "Follow me."

He knew she had no recourse. She'd never been in this section of the castle. The safe was behind a hinged painting, a landscape showing Paradise in better times.

"You don't know the combination. And it might set off an alarm."

"Let me know if the old bastard awakes," said Kaushal. He layered something that looked like clay around the lock.

"What's that?"

"A Wilders' invention." He put a small disk into the moist material. "A gift from Tristan. I've never used this stuff before, so plug your ears."

He tapped the edge of the disk twice, stood back, and plugged his own ears. But there was only a pfft! followed by smoke. The old combination assembly fell to the floor. He ignored the small fortune in gold coins and jewels inside and removed the Golden Scimitar.

"Back to the secret corridors!" he said in a whisper.

***

Twenty minutes later, they covered their mouths to keep from laughing as the castle awoke and everyone started to look for the thieves of the Golden Scimitar.

"One more mission," said Kaushal, when they became more serious.

"What's that?" said Anju.

"A visit to the royal kitchens."

"Won't they be looking there?"

"Not likely. They're far from the First Pilgrim's quarters if you move within the castle. We have a shorter route."

She followed him into the bowels of the castle, a route comprised by many stairways lit by lighting that followed their progress. They stepped through another secret doorway into the cavernous royal kitchens where Kaushal had spent so much time before becoming an entertainer. Some nightlights glowed, but the space was filled with long shadows and dead silence.

"Spooky place. What are you going to do?"

"Poison food supplies."

"Won't that kill cooks and other preparers too?"

"Theoretically, no. They aren't supposed to eat the fancy food intended for the royal elites. Mostly they eat leftovers from their meals. But the chefs will do some tasting and offering samples to kitchen help. So, I'll leave warning notes. I have them already written."

He handed her one. The scrawled note said, "From an old friend who became an entertainer: Please don't eat any of the food you prepare today."

"That's obscure," said Anju.

"It should be warning enough. Many of the staff are from the Second Tribe, and those from the First Tribe are poor devils who don't have any love left for the ruling elites either."

"The king and First Pilgrim aren't stupid. They use tasters."

"This poison won't act fast. Even if Palace Guards doing the tasting start keeling over, it might be too late. Unfortunately, it will be hit or miss. Come and help me."

Kaushal, from his time working in the kitchen, knew where all the storage rooms were. One of his old job's tasks had been to haul baskets and bags of produce and meat from cold storage to the chefs. He handed Anju a dozen syringes.

"Inject the produce nearest the door." He opened the huge refrigerator. "I'll take care of the meat. Hmm. Looks like they're having jonki steaks tomorrow. They've already been filleted."

"Are we going to stick around and watch?" said Anju when they stepped through the secret doorway again.

"I wish we could. No matter if they catch on to our game, it will strike terror in their hearts. Of course, no one will know outside the castle unless we tell them. That's Tristan's mission. Chobi will help. That will happen as soon as we can return."

They left the castle the same way Kaushal had the first time.

***

Anju spotted Royal Guards stationed in front of the pub and grabbed Kaushal's arm.

"They have Chobi!"

Kaushal changed places with her and peered around the corner. "Maybe. It's more likely they're waiting for him."

"Or, he's betrayed us and they're waiting for us."

Anju didn't know Chobi that well, but Kaushal couldn't imagine a betrayal. "The only way he'd do that is if they've tortured him. In that case, he's probably dead by now, his head on a pike. Soldiers always collect their blood money. Can you act like a slut?"

Anju smiled. "This isn't the time for a romantic interlude, my prince."

"I wish. No, I want you to distract the Guards. I can go in through that open side window and get behind them. There are only five, and some are drunk."

"What should I say?"

Kaushal told her. She smiled and moved into the street.

"Are there any men among you?" Anju said to the group, swinging her hips as she approached.

One soldier stepped forward. He had the shiniest boots, so Kaushal knew he was the leader. He headed for the window as the Guard toyed with Anju's dress straps, the others admiring her cleavage.

Inside the pub, Kaushal looked around, saw the kitchen was locked. *No time,* he thought. *I need a weapon.* He then smiled at the irony. Taking the Golden Scimitar from his belt, he stepped onto the boardwalk and attacked the rear soldiers.

Anju went into action too. Kaushal smiled as she tackled a soldier he was dueling with from behind. In seconds, three of the five were bleeding out and the remaining two were unconscious.

"Let's drag them all inside. We'll tie the survivors. I don't feel like killing defenseless people."

When they finished, Anju stood with hands on hip, admiring her handiwork.

"I enjoyed that. Now what do we do?"

"It's possible Chobi and others are bound in the basement where we met earlier. C'mon."

The basement was empty. The old table where they had sat and schemed was still there. Kaushal sat his important cargo on top. He wiped off the Golden Scimitar.

"It's not sharp—" he stopped, seeing Anju's index finger at her lips. He heard steps above them.

"Maybe it was a trap," said Anju.

"We'll hide in that storage closet. Help me gather our loot."

Kaushal was reminded of another near disaster while hiding in a closet. But they had no choice.

Chapter Twenty-Seven

The First Pilgrim's Wrath

"Someone must have seen something!" Gol Kovlyn's fist smashed into the top of his ornate desk. He'd just received the good news the king would survive. Others wouldn't. And he no longer had his symbol of power, the Golden Scimitar. "By the Almighty Ra, I'll have you all beheaded!"

The Captain of the Palace Guards bowed his head. "Sir, we saw no one. We have tortured those who were posted at the entrance of your chambers. We tortured sentries who were posted around lower levels. If they knew anything, they would have spoken to save their lives. I'm sorry, my lord."

"Sorry doesn't cut it. Terrorists have entered the castle and done what they wished. They could have killed me or the king like they killed that fat, old Breman. Triple the number of Palace Guards. We are at siege."

"All is quiet," said the second in command. "Perhaps they entered, did their vile deeds, and now are gone."

"Or, they're hiding, waiting for our complacency to return, when they'll strike again. Triple the number, I say. And not a word of this can ever leave the castle."

Kovlyn hadn't told King Farben the Golden Scimitar was missing. *How can I? It's a holy relic of great importance to our people and a symbol of my power.*

He stood and paced for a moment and then spun and faced the two soldiers, jabbing a fat index finger at them.

"We must find and eliminate these treacherous terrorists. I want every person even remotely suspected to be connected with the opposition on the chopping blocks. I want thousands in the mountains rooting out rebels. I want all Mountain Folk and Wilders exterminated. Do you hear me, you fools?"

"Even if they're from our tribe?" said the captain.

"A traitor is a traitor, whether his ancestors came from Paradise or not." The First Pilgrim smashed a fist into a palm. "It is the Almighty Ra's will, you oaf!"

Kovlyn watched them go. *More importantly, it's my will, as the Almighty Ra's emissary on this wretched planet.*

He glanced skyward and uttered a prayer and then rushed to see how his young king was doing.

***

The First Pilgrim was there when Farben took a turn for the worse. It wasn't a pretty sight as his skin turned yellow and he lost control of bowels and bladder. The king, not much more than an irascible and pampered snot, had become less malleable, but he'd been in the prime of his life. Kovlyn had figured he could control him more as he matured. They had almost reached an understanding. *Poison? It was like the old days back on Paradise!*

He felt no major loss. Farben had possessed no redeeming social qualities—he was worse than his father—but Kovlyn would now need to find a new king. He made a mental survey of the court's remaining nobles and shuddered. They were all incompetent sycophants. And only a few were related to old King Breman in spite of the fat old fool's penchant for augmenting his harem.

"Was it the poison?"

The doctor hesitated. "Can I speak freely, sir?"

Kovlyn shrugged. "Only these four walls, the Almighty Ra, and I are listening. You did the best you could. But I want to know who to blame. Out with it."

"Blame Farben then. He led a life of debauchery. For one so young, you wouldn't believe how many diseases he had acquired, most likely from all those women of ill repute. Mostly VDs, but he also had diabetes and clogged arteries too, unusual for one so young. His gluttonous life exacted its toll. I was told he bedded two prostitutes after a huge dinner. I'm afraid his weakened body couldn't resist the poison as well as others. Both young women survived the poisoning, by the way."

One hedonistic banquet I'm glad I declined to attend. "We can't announce that. We'll execute the women in secret and throw their bodies into the ocean. We'll say he had a congenital heart defect. Does that make sense?"

"Yes, sire. He was a heart attack waiting to happen, but I wouldn't call it congenital. Still, that works for the public."

"He was a believer, after all, a holy man. He will be missed." Kovlyn smiled. "Can you arrange for embalming? We must have a royal funeral."

"Who will ascend the throne?"

Kovlyn thought a moment. "I'll worry about that in good time."

"His future offspring's mother has fled to be with Mountain Folk," said the doctor. "Unless Princess Anju is captured, the direct bloodline no longer exists, as you say. You'll have to choose someone not related to King Breman."

Kovlyn stamped his foot. "I know that, fool. We'll find another even if we have to invent a royal bloodline. People will swallow any lie we feed them. How can they contradict the Almighty Ra's will? They know the king is chosen by Him."

The doctor nodded, turned, and left.

Kovlyn smiled. *If the impudent fool has opinions to the contrary, he keeps them to himself. He values his head. The previous royal physician lost his.*

***

That afternoon, after much scheming, Kovlyn changed his mind. He was tired of kings and the rest of the nobility. Besides, the priesthood outranked them all. They were only window dressing to provide those addicted to pomp and circumstance beyond the ecclesiastical with something to pass the time. He would wait a bit for the funeral, say Farben had been murdered, like Breman, and declare martial law. His campaign to find the traitors to the Almighty Ra, Isis, and Osiris, would be justified by the murders of Breman and Farben. *Maybe our realm doesn't need nobility!*

The young boy lying on his bed was reading a book. Kovlyn admired the naked figure. He was the picture of innocence. Black hair and rosy cheeks framed his cherubic face. There was only a hint of pubic hair. He had watched the Guard strip the lad, licking his lips in anticipation. *I'm so stressed. Time for some rest and relaxation.*

Kovlyn went to the bed, disrobed, and lay down beside the twelve-year-old. Hours later, when they were through, Palace Guards entered and removed the lad. They would take him somewhere and execute him. No one, not even a child, could look upon the First Pilgrim's naked body and live to tell the tale, a policy in existence since the Founder's time. The First Pilgrim was the Almighty Ra incarnate, after all.

His stress was diminished, so sleep came easily.

Part Six

A War of Words

Throughout the history of near-Earth planets, achieving public support with well-chosen words has been as effective as military might. This is why tyrants like to control public discourse. Knowledge is power. If the public doesn't know what's going on, they aren't willing to fight. And a ruler who loses the public's trust is a fool.

— Jenny Wong, an important figure in the history of ITUIP

Chapter Twenty-Eight

Competing Propaganda

Kaushal was in front of Anju in the storage closet.

"You're getting hard, my Prince."

"Difficult not to, although you're not naked. Your straps are broken, you know."

Anju covered herself. "Get us out of this scrape, and I will reward you tonight."

"I accept the offer," he said with a smile. He gripped the Scimitar.

When he heard boots stop in front of the closet, he threw the door open and raised the weapon. A strong arm stopped the descent.

"Stop!" said Chobi. "It's me and Tristan."

Tristan peered over the big man's shoulder. "I see bags of loot. Missions completed?"

Kaushal and Anju stepped out.

"We were worried that bad things happened here," said Anju.

"Informants told us that squadron was on its way," said Chobi. "Someone in the neighborhood betrayed us, likely for part of the reward. We were watching, knowing you'd return here. We saw you two make short work of the king's men. Well done!"

"Farben's dead, by the way," said Tristan. "The First Pilgrim has declared a state of emergency and martial law. Hundreds are being rounded up. I expect guilt will be assumed before innocence. Kovlyn is looking for blood."

"Now you can make your announcement to counter his lies," said Anju, still holding onto her bodice.

"I only need give the word," said Chobi. "Some elders will be here and bear witness that we have the Scimitar."

"It was a help in that fight," said Kaushal with a smile, "even if it is ceremonial."

***

By week's end, Anju, Kaushal, and Tristan were back in the mountains and most of Eden knew the First Pilgrim was a liar. His purge continued, though. Public beheadings were a daily occurrence. At first, First Tribe gawkers attended, but when they saw friends and relatives go on the chopping blocks too, the crowds diminished and the opposition started to grow, even among First Tribesmen. Executions diminished as the resistance became more adept at hiding people.

Chobi smiled at a First Tribesman as he sat the tankard in front of his client. "Lots of conflicting news," he said.

The man shrugged. "My cousin has a friend in the Second Tribe who saw the Scimitar. If the First Pilgrim lies about having it still, he can lie about anything. I don't know what to do. The Almighty Ra has deserted us."

"Maybe the Almighty Ra's tired of the First Pilgrim's lies too," said Chobi.

"I'll drink to that. I don't know what to do about all this. Royal Guards captured another cousin, accusing her of treason to the king and First Pilgrim. We buried her yesterday. They raped and murdered her. At least they didn't behead her and put her head on a pike."

"Don't think that's because she was a woman. I've seen their heads too. I don't know what to do either. I keep selling my liquor, hoping things will be better."

"That's a bit irresponsible," the customer said. He leaned forward. "I need to find people who want to do something about it. You don't happen to know anyone, do you?"

"Maybe I do and maybe I don't. And maybe I don't want to be involved. I only run a pub."

"Come on. Pub owners hear a lot of gossip. I bet you know how I can connect with the right people."

"Because I'm from the Second Tribe?"

"Because you're fed up with the First Pilgrim and his murdering soldiers like me," said the customer.

Chobi handed the First Tribesman a piece of paper with two cross streets written on it. "Be at that corner at midnight."

After the fellow left, another man who'd been sitting in the corner pretending to sleep, rose and approached Chobi.

"A candidate?" he said.

"Maybe," said Chobi. He summarized what the other customer had said. "Confirm his story. If there's even one little lie, slit his throat when he appears on that street corner. Otherwise, work him into a cell that doesn't have any critical assignments yet. We can test him that way."

***

"We're winning the propaganda war," Tristan said to his inner circle of conspirators. "People are joining our cause."

"Don't we have to watch for spies?" said Anju.

"Yes, but the cell structure helps there," said Kaushal. "The average conspirator only knows people in his cell. The leaders of only a few cells know each other and a higher echelon leader. It's an old technique."

"We also vet our new members and have everyone watch everyone else," said Tristan. "In a few days, the real fun begins."

"What's that?" said Kaushal.

"We will start destroying the First Pilgrim's manpower base and infrastructure. He won't have an infinite number of thugs to do his dirty work. He also won't have infinite supplies or a reliable supply chain. The farther from the capital a farmer is, the less he wants to feed the soldiers. Same for factories. All of Eden knows the First Pilgrim is a liar now."

"Not having the Scimitar when he says he does goes a long way toward establishing that," said Anju, "but I have something else on the great man that might be of use."

Kaushal raised an eyebrow. "I thought I knew all your secrets."

She blushed and laughed. "It never occurred to me to use the information before, so I didn't mention it, that's all. But now I understand how negative propaganda works. We're trying to ruin the reputation of the Almighty Ra's mouthpiece here on Eden, right?" They nodded. "I have something that will do that maybe even more than the loss of the Scimitar, at least for some."

"Give," said Tristan.

"The First Pilgrim likes little boys. Worse, he abuses them and then murders them."

"I find that hard to believe," said Kaushal, mouth agape. "He can't be that evil!"

"Considering people are being beheaded for little reason at all," said Tristan, "that's a surprising statement from you." He turned to Anju. "How do we confirm that?"

"My word's not enough?" said Anju.

Kaushal nodded. "Enough for us, but, like the Scimitar, we have to show people and start them talking about it. That would undermine his moral authority more than losing the Scimitar, which only took away the symbol of being the Founder's anointed."

"A video recorder," said Tristan. "We need to record one of his trysts."

"Too risky," said Anju. "Last time he was asleep. He can summon Palace Guards if he's awake and enjoying himself in bed."

"That's the trick!" said Kaushal, snapping his fingers. "One of them knows what's going on. When not on duty, they're in barracks outside the castle, unless they have wives or children. A spy can get the list of those who are the First Pilgrim's personal bodyguards. We'll find one who knows all about the holy man's predilection for little boys and make him reveal all."

"Why would he do that?" said Tristan. "He'd be signing his death warrant."

"We'll make him assume that if he doesn't, he's signing his death warrant with us."

***

Kaushal and Tristan made the trip along mountain trails into Angels' Bay to explain the plan to Chobi. Meeting once again in the pub's basement, the pub owner had another revelation.

"We heard that story," he said. "It made us think Ravik was a spy at first when he told us because it seemed so farfetched. We couldn't confirm it either. But Ravik proved his worth in other ways."

"Who's Ravik?" said Tristan.

"About the ugliest man you'll ever meet. Other Palace Guards call him The Beast."

"So, he's a member of the Royal Guard on duty in the palace? That's a major worry. He might be a spy!"

"In the First Pilgrim's special elite group of Palace Guards," said Chobi with a nod. "One of the higher ranking fellows. I trust him. I thought of asking him to kill the First Pilgrim, and he'd do it, but that would be a suicide mission. Instead, he's a great spy for us. We have good intel on what Kovlyn is doing now." He thought a moment. "So, it's true. And that fat priest is always preaching about the sin of lusting after someone of the same sex. He's a hypocrite besides being an evil despot."

"Worse," said Kaushal. "He rapes and murders little boys."

"Yes, that's a lot more than homosexuality," said Tristan. He saw Kaushal's raised eyebrows. "I'm not implying the latter is bad or good. Different cultures interpret it differently, and it's not my place to pass judgment, only to study it as another interesting variation of Human sexuality." Kaushal nodded his agreement. "But back to exploiting Kovlyn's evil habit. Too bad we have so few video receiving sets. Only the rich can afford them."

"And all you find in the transmissions is propaganda and religious diatribes from the First Pilgrim, along with travelogues extolling the planet's natural vistas as a gift from Nut," said Chobi. They looked at him, all thinking the same thing. "I never saw your so-called videos, but Ravik told us about what they are, who has them, and what they watch."

"Forget the videos," said Kaushal. "Have Ravik tell his story to a bunch of cell leaders. They can pass the word. It will spread as fast as other propaganda."

"A two-pronged attack is better," said Tristan. "Let's film Ravik with a mask to hide his face and disguise his voice and then hack into their video network and show the film to the nobles of the court. Can't hurt. Some will be disgusted and outraged."

"Or worse," said Chobi, nodding. "I don't understand much what you're saying, but it sounds good. And a whole lot of fun. How do we do that?"

Tristan told them.

Chapter Twenty-Nine

The Sermon

Chobi's crew brought the boat near the seawall again although the ocean was rougher this time. It took three shots before the grappling hook grabbed the sill of the old castle window. *Had his father's soldiers shot their cannons and breechloaders at marauding pirates from those bastions?* It was no place for archers because they would be ineffective against ships and sailors for lack of range. Kaushal couldn't remember anything like that being discussed, but why would they discuss it around a small boy?

He scaled the cliff and castle wall for the second time and entered. The first part was more difficult this time—spray from crashing waves had made the rocks slippery. The stone wall of the building's seawall was easier, grooves between mortared stones providing recesses for the toes of his boots.

Anju had been too pregnant to accompany him this time. She didn't argue about being left behind, but she made him promise to be careful. He smiled. *If they kill me, she will never forgive me!* He thought it special to be loved by someone so much that she would worry until he returned. It motivated him to be careful as well as successful. *I shall return to her!*

They still hadn't resolved the issue of Kifi, Ezan, and Kiana. He loved them all, but Anju was his first love. But he was coming around to the idea harems among Eden's nobility were more evidence for the decadence and evil of the theocracy. *But I never paid much attention to that aspect of New*

Haven society. He should have. It might be a good model to emulate when he became king.

These philosophical thoughts ended when he swung through the open window. He became focused on his mission. He disappeared into his secret corridors. *What would we have done if I didn't know these passageways?* That thought also bolstered him. He was sure the road to his future was destined to lead to the First Pilgrim's downfall. *Is that what it means to be a follower of the Way? No, that might be arrogance!*

At one point, he detected cooking odors from the palace kitchens. *Who's doing the cooking now? Has all Second Tribe staff been replaced?* He knew Farben had deserved to die, but his old friends hadn't. He hoped most of them had escaped. He wrinkled his nose and tried to ignore the culinary scents.

He had no problem finding the video studio. It wasn't far from his electronic junk room. At one time, his father's technicians probably used both and more. The First Pilgrim only used technology as a tool to manipulate the masses, passing off results as religious miracles and magic. They made him the Royal Mage.

He replaced a data cube labeled as the next day's sermon for the faithful—that meant noble sycophants in the court, whose faith often played a secondary role in their struggle for power—with Ravik's description of the holy man's hobby. He peeled off the original label and stuck it on the opposition's cube. He pocketed the real sermon for later destruction. He counted on the projectionist to plug, play, and leave for a time—the First Pilgrim's sermons tended to be verbose, repetitive, and boring.

He made sure everything looked the same as when he entered and headed back the way he came. It should have been an easy in-and-out job, but not far from the studio a Palace Guard surprised him. Kaushal had no weapon. The burly man threw him against the corridor's stone wall and held the edge of his broadsword to Kaushal's throat.

"I know you. You're that entertainer. They want you for questioning about the death of King Breman."

"I knew they did, so I didn't stick around," said Kaushal. *I'm not about to admit anything to this oaf.* "Would you have stayed?" He eyed the keen blade now showing a trickle of blood across its broad surface.

The Guard relaxed a little. Kaushal pushed the flat part of the blade away with his hand, kneed the soldier in the groin, and floored him with an uppercut. Shaking his hand from the pain—the giant had a brick for a chin—he retrieved the broadsword with his uninjured hand and put the tip to the man's throat. He thanked Wilders for training him to use either hand when wielding a sword. He managed to hold it steady, although it made the Golden Scimitar seem like a child's toy.

"It's your unlucky day," said Kaushal, "finding me here. I can't let you live. But tell me your name, and we will tell your family you died nobly."

"An entertainer who knows how to fight. Who figured? My name is Ravik." He tensed for the coup de grace.

Kaushal pulled the sword away and doubled up laughing. The hirsute fellow rose and stared at him in wonder.

"You still have my sword, but I'll dare ask: what's so funny? Or, have you gone daft?"

"My friend, we've just discovered a weakness in the cell system. You have no idea who I am, do you?"

"That entertainer. I told you that. Kovlyn wants your head. I'm surprised to see you here. Are you as deaf as you are daft, lad?"

"More than entertainer, Ravik. I'm Prince Kaushal, one of the opposition leaders."

Ravik looked astonished but recovered. He dropped to his right knee and inclined his head. "I had heard rumors. You're the true king."

"Rise, Ravik. You'll never have to bow to me again. I'll not hear of it. And I'm no one's king yet. Maybe never."

"But why did they send you? It's risky. Surely they need to keep you safe. And what are you doing here?"

"So many questions, so little time. As Hach Merson's son and, yes, that entertainer, I know this castle better than the back of my hand. You will soon be famous, Ravik. Not identified as Ravik, but still famous. That's a promise I can keep."

"The video?" said Ravik with a grin.

"Good guess. Please keep all this to yourself." He returned the sword to Ravik. "Why were you here?"

"It's called a sweep. Before the First Pilgrim goes anywhere in the castle now, we scout ahead and make sure it's safe. He's paranoid after what happened with the Scimitar and King Farben. I don't care if he's safe, of course, but I keep up the pretense. I have to. He'll be here in a bit to record day-after-tomorrow's sermon. It's always a production, with his magic often thrown in to fool the people."

"And you'll tell him the area is clear, please. Don't mention my name. We want tomorrow's sermon to be broadcast right on schedule. Now I must go." He put a hand on the ugly giant's shoulder. "You are doing noble work, but I won't tell your family about it, my friend. At least, not until some serious changes are made on Eden."

Ravik grinned again.

***

"You took long enough," Chobi said as Kaushal swung on the rope and descended onto the boat's deck. He had chosen to leave the castle that way this time as a precaution. In this spy business, creatures of habit didn't survive long. The old sailor and pub owner steadied him. "I was worried."

Kaushal soon recovered his sea legs although the boat was tossing and turning in the wild surf. He stared up at the window and smiled.

"We might need to revise how we're organized," he said. "Ravik almost killed me. I could have killed him too."

"You're kidding. We hadn't thought of that. What a coincidence!"

"Coincidences can be deadly. But everyone makes mistakes. Even Tristan. I'm sure he read about the cell organization somewhere and thought it was a good idea. We'll have to modify it. Never mind for now. We're all set. Let's put out to sea."

"How is this all going to end?" said Chobi as he handed Kaushal a pipe a half-hour later.

Kaushal lit the pipe, all the time scanning around, enjoying the blue sky and roiling waters. No land in sight. He loved the sea more than ever. It was like a peaceful haven, considering all the scheming and strife on land. *Did Father enjoy the sea too?* It would seem so, considering Starlight Castle was built between sea and sky. He realized how little he knew about his father. How could he remedy that? Not easily, to be sure.

He blew smoke and watched the stiff breeze whip it across the waves. He suspected the fine Wilders tobacco was imported by smugglers who had succeeded Chobi. At his pub, you sometimes could order the day's special and have a feast fit for nobility. As an ex-gofer for the royal kitchens, he had sampled some of those feasts. He decided Chobi's cook had access to better ingredients.

"End? I hope soon. For us, this has gone on too long, ever since we took the First Tribe in. My father was naïve and paid for it. We're not naïve, but we have fought and will fight bloody battles to change things back to how they were before."

"I've heard rumors you've been to better places out there," said Chobi, jerking a thumb toward the heavens. "Why did you come back? Anything must be better than here."

"There are people I love here, friends and family, and the whole planet is suffering from an oppressive theocracy." He winked. "And maybe for revenge."

"What's theocracy mean?"

"It means having despots pretending to be the Almighty Ra's anointed who exploit, torture, rape, and murder ordinary people in the name of religion. I learned many things from my mother and not enough from my father, but out there I learned what's happening here has happened before. Even before men and women migrated to the stars, it was a common occurrence."

"How long ago was that?" said Chobi.

"I'm not sure. Thousands of years, I suppose. And we're not alone. War and strife are common among other beings as they reach for the stars."

"Religion is only the excuse," said Chobi. "Power and greed are the real motivators." Kaushal smiled at his deduction. "Will you become our new king?"

"Do you want me to?"

"I'm not sure putting all that power in one man's hands is good. Even if that man is you."

Kaushal nodded. "You might be on to something, esteemed friend. Before we become too philosophical, I think I see the cove off Dragon's Head."

"You have a sailor's eyes," said Chobi.

He gave the order to head for land.

Part Seven

New Tactics

When you lose a battle, it is time to assess your failure and make changes. Repeating the same errors isn't advisable...and you might not live too long that way.

—Trevor Morgan, the emancipator of Earth

Chapter Thirty

Plans Are Made

They had agreed to meet in the encampment in the mountains near Dragon's Head. Kifi, Ezan, Kiana, and Tristan were waiting for them.

"It's good to see you again," said Kifi, punching Kaushal lightly in the stomach and then kissing him on the cheek.

Kaushal held her at arm's length, noticing the white scar across her bare midriff. "I'm happy to see you again too. I'd feared the worst." He turned to Ezan and saw the empty eye socket. "You too. You were lucky."

Ezan kissed him on the cheek too. "In a way, yes. I'm not dead, only disfigured."

Kaushal held her at arm's length too. "It's what's in the heart that counts," he said. "Are you with your husband?"

"He died in battle, Kaushal."

"I'm sorry. I'm sure he was a good man. He had to be. He chose you."

"Tristan, don't we have business to attend to?" said Kiana.

"I was about to make a comment to that effect," said Tristan. "I'm glad to know you were successful."

"I guess we have no way to watch nobles' reactions when they see the video," said Chobi.

"Or the First Pilgrim's," said Kaushal. "But our spies will bring us word. The video might be the tipping point. I hope Ravik will be OK."

Tristan nodded. "He only knew you as the entertainer, and you'd never seen his face before, so don't be guilty. We nearly had a disaster, though. We need to rethink how we organize a bit. The current system needs improvement."

"What's to rethink?" said Ezan. "Aren't we going to attack that drax Kovlyn and his Royal Guards? Everyone's on our side now, or soon will be."

"Let's discuss that for a while," said Tristan, motioning toward a large tent. "Both organization and how to continue the good fight. We need to ensure success this time."

Kaushal noticed all three women sat together. As they talked, he also noticed them smiling at him when their eyes met. *I'm in trouble now!* He forced himself to focus on what people were saying.

Tristan led the discussion. Chobi had joined other sentries to brag about his adventures with Kaushal. An older man named Pel sat on Tristan's left, Kaushal on his right. Three men and three women would try to create a successful plan to save the world.

***

Pel was a Wilder. Mountain Folk called him The General. Although he knew other Wilder leaders, Samos and Kindri, Pel was something of a mystic. A devout follower of the Way, he had no use for the First Pilgrim or his Almighty Ra. The reclusive old man had descended from his hideout near Dragon's Mountain to join with those who attacked Angels' Bay. He decided to stay around afterward to support and motivate the defeated. He was now leader in this small encampment.

"I predict the First Pilgrim will go into a rage when he sees the video," Pel said. "The people will suffer more, but that's when he'll be the most vulnerable. Good work, Prince Kaushal."

Kaushal didn't like his formality. *Or is he only being polite?* He would have to set him straight about using that title. He noticed Kiana picked up on it. She knew him well enough to sense he often was uncomfortable playing the role of a cultural icon.

"Which is why we should attack!" said Ezan.

"That didn't work so well before," said Pel. "We need to do that, of course, figuring more people will support us now. But, after hearing Kaushal had entered the castle twice, we can also do something else."

"A commando raid inside the castle?" said Kifi.

"Precisely. I doubt the First Pilgrim will be outside leading the Guards. He's old, fat, and frail. He'll have his Palace Guard contingent protecting him, of course, but if we capture him now, it's all over. No one, not even nobles of the realm, will support him."

Kaushal thought a moment. "I'll have to go, of course, because I know the castle so well. Anju's not able to do so, and I wouldn't let her go. We need to pick my team carefully and keep its members a secret. I need one team trained in battle to sail with me as a minimum."

"Chobi?" said Kiana.

"Too old," said Tristan. "The commandoes have to hit hard and fast. At night and high tide."

"We need some insurance against failure," said Kaushal. "I'd also like to add to Kifi and Pel's proposal."

***

"Pel deserves his nickname," Kaushal said to Tristan after the others had left the tent to prepare their meager dinners. They still had many details to work out, but Kaushal was pleased with the results. He was worried about the old man, though.

"He's a wise one," said Tristan. "He's led many Humans into battle. He knows about ITUIP, by the way."

"How's he know?"

"He's older than he looks. Off-planet Humans can take longevity drugs and live for a long time."

"I guess I never understood that when I was on New Haven, attributing it to better healthcare—or maybe I heard about it and had my mind on other things. Kiana reminded me on Quick Death. Longer lives might be good if it makes people value life more. It would also slow things down. We're living at a hectic pace here on Eden." Kaushal thought a bit. "But are you saying Pel isn't one of us?"

"I'm not sure. Maybe he was born here, went away, and then returned?"

"How'd he break through quarantine?"

"It wasn't enforced all that well when Eden belonged to the Second Tribe and the First Tribe was on Paradise. I imagine he's been here at least that long."

Hundreds of years! "Why don't we ask him about his history?" said Kaushal.

"One thing you have to learn, Kaushal, is to value a person's privacy. If he thinks it's important for us to know, he'll tell us."

"Did you take longevity drugs too?" said Kaushal.

"You know I'm not from here," said Tristan.

"I'll take that as a yes,' said Kaushal. *Damned guy is always so mysterious.* "I guess my worry is whether we can trust Pel. I don't know him that well. He seems to be a mystic too, talking in riddles a bit. Can he fight?"

"Better than most, my friend. Like I said, he's led many into battle. Shall we go see what's for dinner?"

"It's always jonki this, jonki that," said Kaushal with a laugh. Not that he minded—it beat what the poor ate in the outskirts of Angels' Bay. He hoped to remedy that problem some day.

***

Pel treated them to a Wilders' dance after their meager dinners. Kiana and some Mountain Folk joined in, trying to follow his steps and undulations. Kaushal didn't stay long, wandering off into the night until music and laughter began to fade into the murmuring background created by mountain creatures.

"Altitude makes them brighter," said Ezan, approaching Kaushal after finding him staring at the stars. She sat beside him and hugged herself. "It also increases the cold at night."

Kaushal frowned, remembering his friend Benish's explanation so long ago inside that mountain cave.

"You've been hanging around Tristan too much," said Kaushal as Kifi followed Ezan to sit on the granite ledge at his other side. "He's always making some scientific explanation about something. It always sounds reasonable, but I can't tell if it's true most of the time."

"That's Tristan, I'll agree," said Kifi. "He's also one secretive fellow, like you with your adventures away from Eden. Kiana told us some of the story."

"Where is she?"

"She and Pel are discussing something. What is it like out there?"

"Space? Stars? All hard to describe. It's a bit like the ocean. Maybe 'cold, desolate beauty' are the correct words." He wrapped an arm around Kifi's waist. "Not like you two."

He was surprised when she pulled away. "We have to talk," she said.

"Kifi and I are a pair now," said Ezan.

Kaushal's eyebrows raised. He took her literally, although it wasn't common. "I didn't see that coming. I'll admit I've seen you two enjoy each other, but we were a frolicking threesome in the Southlands at the time."

"Ezan lost her husband. That changed things." Kifi smiled at her.

Ezan was hugging herself and rocking. "No, we finally came to our senses," she said with a smile. "We still love you, Kaushal, but differently now. We've changed. Better said, we discovered who we are, and we need each other. Besides, you now have your true love back."

"She was OK with Kiana. She's also OK with you two. There was no problem there."

"I'm sorry," said Kifi. "Will you forgive us?"

"There's nothing to forgive. I love you too much not to respect your choices. Life is too short to do otherwise." *But the pain will linger.*

"That's settled then," said Ezan, giving him a kiss on the cheek.

Kifi kissed him on the other cheek. The two women left. He went back to staring at stars, but his eyes were moist now, blurring them into a diffuse band. He was like a patient after a surgeon had removed several essential body parts.

***

"You're an early riser," said Tristan, crouching and ladling some light tea made from tree bark into his mug. "Good to know you can cook."

"I can boil water and steep bark," said Kaushal. "I also know the theory. I watched expert castle cooks prepare meals for the nobles, remember. They let me try my hand at it sometimes." He spotted a naked Kiana leaving Pel's tent to disappear into the brush to tend to bodily functions. He shook his head. "My harem has been reduced to one."

Tristan followed his line of sight and laughed. "One never stops learning, lad. There's nothing more mysterious than women. And there's nothing I understand less than Human sexuality. Would you prefer to have them happy or slavishly serving your needs?"

"Happy, of course. You knew about Kifi and Ezan?" Tristan nodded. "I suppose I shouldn't be surprised. They were always close. They were close even when Ezan's husband was alive. And I was gone a long time after he died."

"The duration of your trip had nothing to do with it. When you understand the Way more, you'll realize no one can or should bend others' lives into what suits his or her selfish purposes. Others have the right to follow their own paths."

"That's a good credo. What about Kiana? I knew something was going on when I saw how Pel and she danced together. What does she see in Pel?"

"You say that because Pel is old? So is Kiana. They chose to stop their aging in different places in their lives. You were worried about Pel, so I chatted with them. They are the only Humans I know who remember Earth as it was before the Tali invasion. That information is confidential, by the way."

"How old are they?"

Tristan shrugged. "Thousands of standard years. It doesn't matter. They're here to help us. They're a team, but Pel goes to his mountain hideout when Kiana is off-planet. Kiana is Pel's wife."

"What? She would betray her husband? We were lovers!"

"Did Ezan betray her husband? Not if she told him about you. Openness isn't betrayal. I've seen stranger behaviors among Humans, and let's not go there with other sentients. One can explain it all away by evolution—a lifeform's sexual practices have evolved over millions of years in order to ensure its success in the particular planetary environmental niche it inhabits. Human sexuality is still a great mystery to me no matter how long I study it. In stressful times, temporary relationships often flourish. People might go mad without some comfort."

Kaushal nodded. That lecture wasn't atypical. Tristan was a philosopher. "I have a lot to learn. So, what's your story? You're a strange one, always talking about Humans as if we're some strange biological specimens you put under a microscope."

Tristan smiled. "Only in comparison to Rangers, Talis, and so forth. All sentient beings are interesting."

"Are you from Earth?"

"In a way. We should start slicing some jonki bacon. People are stirring. They'll need a solid breakfast to get over their hangovers."

Chapter Thirty-One

The Commandoes

Pel floored Kaushal with ease but then offered a hand up.

"Disguise your moves, lad. An opponent can use what's coming against you."

Kaushal nodded. "Ezan and Kifi taught me some hand-to-hand combat techniques, but I've been delinquent in honing my skills. That was a move I hadn't seen, though."

Pel was surprisingly nimble and limber. Kaushal had started to believe Tristan's stories about him.

"Let me teach it to you." He spent some more moments working with Kaushal, and then waved Kifi over. "Now it's your turn."

After going through the warriors selected to be commandoes, Pel left them to practice in pairs.

***

"Will they be ready?" Tristan said, watching them go at it. They were holding back on moves that would be lethal to a real opponent, of course. That already took skill. And they could ill afford to lose one of their own in practice before going into battle.

"We might find better candidates among Wilders," said Pel, "but the answer to your question is yes. Combat here on Eden has one advantage over combat elsewhere."

"What's that? It's very primitive?"

Pel shook his head. "The mix of old and new weaponry and the dearth of the latter often makes warfare more personal, that's true, but, because life is short, people know their time will eventually come. They go all out. Of course, that affects both sides, so motivation comes in play." He winked. "With longevity drugs, people are overly cautious sometimes." *I've overcome that.*

"But medical care is far better. That should compensate, don't you think?"

"Still, it's good ITUIP forces rarely have to fight face-to-face. A porta-doc isn't always nearby. Of course, to followers of the Way, it's all moot—what will be, will be. Even with longevity, nothing lasts forever."

"You're doing a good job. You're highly motivated. There was a time when you lost the Way. What happened?"

"I lost my first loves," said Pel. "I suppose that sounds like sentimental jonki crap, but it's the truth. Of course, I eventually recovered Kiana. Nevertheless, I worry for Kaushal. He's had some emotional blows recently. That can kill one's motivation."

"Kifi and Ezan were his number two and three, Kiana his number four. He'll be fine with Anju once he's able to organize his mind and come to terms. They seem to be destined for each other, if the Way permits such statements."

"Destiny can be fickle," said Pel. He did some squats and head movements to keep limber. "We'll see how it works out. She's carrying that beast's son too. That might be tough for both of them."

"I'm glad those kind of emotions don't haunt me," said Tristan.

Pel smiled. Tristan was reason and logic incarnate, a philosopher's philosopher.

***

The training course continued. In three weeks, Pel gave them a final exam. By the end, Kaushal felt sorry for the old man. They couldn't take him down a lot, but he was thrown to the hard ground a few times. He always bounced up with a smile on his face. *It must be rewarding to see a pupil take your teaching to heart.*

They moved on to the second step in the training: how to use the weapons they had available. This also included cases where an opponent had a particular weapon and the commando didn't. Members of the group had experience with weapons, but the second case was more difficult.

Skills were honed, physiques improved, and mental focus sharpened. At the end of another four weeks, Pel was satisfied. They divided the commandoes into two groups for the two-pronged attack on the castle.

During those seven weeks, Eden's other rebel forces were also organizing and training. Pel and Kiana would lead Mountain Folk. Their old friends, Samos and Kindri, would lead Wilders. The latter forces would move once again on New Hope and Long Beach, now reclaimed by the opposition. The garrisons were still weak, though, but the whole southern campaign would be more difficult this time. Their opponents would be more prepared, and rebels would lose most of the element of surprise. On the other hand, the First Pilgrim had lost all respect, so infiltrating the three target cities would be less difficult. Rebels would be welcomed with open arms even by First Tribesmen.

***

Kaushal surprised Anju with a quick visit. He feared two things: she would give birth without him by her side, and he would die in battle, never being able to be with her again. He didn't talk about those fears, though, only a better future for them and the baby to come.

"I guess I'd better stick around," she said as he slathered oil onto her belly. "Your harem has shrunk to just one woman. Is our little friend getting no exercise now?"

He smiled. "If you're asking whether he misses Kifi, Ezan, and Kiana, the answer is yes. Knowing they are happy is compensation, though."

"That's noble of you, my prince. But I'm only asking if you missed me."

"I wouldn't be here if I didn't. Being here is special."

"And restful. I love those women too, you know. They deserve happiness." She patted her belly. "The little jonki is kicking."

"I know. I feel him too. You'll be fine here in the mountains. Kifi swears by the Mountain Folk's midwives. I wish I were king already so I could provide some royal physicians for you, though."

"I'll be fine. Humans have been having babies for a long time, you know. A midwife or physician is often superfluous. And I wouldn't want the First Tribe's physicians touching me. They're just sycophants like the court's nobles."

He gave her a kiss. "This time we'll succeed. We have embellished strategies, created new ones, and we're physically better prepared to fight. We'll win. I feel it in my bones."

"When you return from the campaign, we'll give our little friend his rewards," said Anju. "You will be careful, won't you?"

"We've trained so well I can fight in my sleep," he said. He stared past her. "I'm wondering what I should do afterwards."

"You mean, as king? That should be obvious. Rule, my husband. Turn Eden into a world of free and generous people, ready to join the rest of the galaxy."

"Join ITUIP? That will be a longer battle still. They have every reason to be cautious."

"I suppose. But you've already started that campaign. Pel, Kiana, and Tristan will help. It's our destiny."

He finished and lay down beside her. "I'm going to abdicate the throne. Having a privileged and poor class is impractical as well as unconscionable. We need a fairer distribution of wealth and the people to rule."

"The people will need a king for a while. Maybe you can evolve that duty to where your role is largely ceremonial. A sudden break in tradition might be a culture shock for them."

"But it might help with joining ITUIP. When merchants come and people's lives improve, they will no longer need a royal family and their sycophants. I want to return to space, Anju, with you and our little ones. There are many worlds to see."

"Sounds exciting. Give me another kiss, and let's sleep on it."

Chapter Thirty-Two
The First Pilgrim's Depression

Gol Kovlyn could understand some of the unrest in his domain. He was a spiritual leader, not a king, after all, so he could follow social threads in the capital's complex tapestry of opinion.

Those outside the court wanted a king, hopefully a better one, but nobles clamored for one, better or not. Their fawning and jockeying for position irked him. But with the Scimitar gone and his predilection for underage boys now common knowledge, there were many who thought he should resign as First Pilgrim. He no longer had any moral authority, they said. He was also losing political authority as martial law became more despotic.

He continued with his sermons, but spies informed him they often fell on deaf ears now. Some superstitious dolts were still impressed with the sermons' beginnings— they still put on a good show with the special effects technology, one befitting a message from the King's Mage. But how many old believers in his magic now thought his powers had their genesis in evil? Instigators among the population encouraged that belief. The number of his enemies and doubters was growing.

Today forty accused of treason to the realm stood on the execution platforms. Nine were women, three adolescents. Over half the group was from the First Tribe. *Sinners all,* he thought. *To defy my authority is to sin against the Almighty Ra, Isis, Osiris, and the Founder.* He watched the sharp scimitars descend followed by gushing blood and heads rolling into baskets. *Would they receive salvation?* He thought not. They would be damned for eternity, as they should be.

He turned away from the window after watching the executions, the only reason being that they were boring—he had become calloused to blood and gore. *What are Wilders up to now?* They never saved anyone anymore. He headed for the chapel where a eunuch from the Second Tribe helped him kneel and stepped back to wait for him to finish praying.

He didn't trust the Palace Guards now and wouldn't be alone with them. *The man in the video must be one of them! He knew too much.* He had thought of putting all Guards who had the size and build of that lout to death, but it wasn't practical—most Palace Guards possessed a similar size and build. So he trusted them only when other nobles were present and being guarded. *I'd still like to find that man in the video!*

He glanced back at the eunuch. *Why trust them?* In some sense, they had more reason to complain about those in power, but they had shown no signs of being aware of what was going on outside the castle. *How can they be?* They'd lived their whole lives inside in service to the court. Some had been lads he had defiled, a reward for his having a good time; others had been chosen by priests in Angels' Bay. And he had to trust someone or become a paranoid recluse.

"Lord Almighty Ra, All Powerful and from Whom All Blessings Flow, give me the strength to survive these trials. May Isis and Osiris, your son and daughter sitting on your left and right, also smile upon me and give me peace, and may Nut, who gave us Paradise and Eden, continue to bless us with her favors. I won't ask what I've done to deserve these trials, although I feel I'm innocent of any wrongdoings. I will strive to make this planet Your domain, Your world, a place where all bow before you on pain of death. Heretics and sinners will be punished, or I will die trying. If Your will is for that to happen, I pray I can fly home to be welcomed into Your loving arms, embrace Your royal children, and partake of Your dark and eternal mysteries. Amen."

He rose. The eunuch brought forward wafers and wine. He would take them, bless them, and eat and drink, and the Almighty Ra would bless his prayer. It was a bit of ceremonial order in all the chaos.

**

Another day of worry began. Some nobles paraded through, offering and receiving advice, but most were only loyal sycophants who figured they had more to lose if the rebels won. And rebels there were; their numbers growing every day.

When the last one left, he started to pace. He did a lot of pacing now. Public sentiment was against him. Although armed forces at his command followed his orders, he knew there was unrest among them too. *What is their state of morale? Will they fight for me when attacked?*

Kovlyn knew attacks would come. Already rebels were busy destroying his infrastructure. Food was also scarce now because shipping and caravans were being attacked too. The farther away one ventured from Angels' Bay, the more dangerous it became for anyone favoring the old, privileged order. He could imagine his head on the chopping block one day and shuddered.

He lit some incense and left the throne room. *I need one of my cherubic young lads to give me some comfort.*

**

Kovlyn awoke with a start. He was sweating. *Bad dream!* He rose and noticed the little angel sleeping next to him. The boy had sung to him in a clear and beautiful soprano voice. *I won't have this one killed.* He knew it didn't matter anymore, though; his secret was out.

He bathed, dressed, and returned to his study.

"I'll dine on the balcony," he told another eunuch.

The eunuch gave a little bow and disappeared. A half-hour later, dinner was served. He had an appetite and enjoyed the meal.

He was content and folded his hands across his immense girth. *I will win. The Almighty Ra has anointed me! He has chosen me to represent Him and his blessed progeny, Isis and Osiris.*

He watched some barges move through Angels' Bay into the river and the sun setting over the mountains, and then looked to the sky to see that huge ribbon of stars as night fell. Some said men's original planet was somewhere not far from Eden, the original home of Nut, the goddess and maker of all planets. It was fortunate the Founder had convinced the Almighty Ra and his entourage to follow them to Paradise and Eden. They would have become lost among the stars. Here they were protected.

The stars disappeared as a large dark object first descended but then moved on over the castle. He shivered. *Is it Osiris or an avenging angel of the Almighty Ra? No, I have done nothing wrong!*

He hurried inside. But nothing happened the remainder of the night. He didn't sleep well, so he ventured into the vaults where the Founder and others lay in state. The original First Pilgrim looked alive but floating in the cold mists of the sarcophagus. The current First Pilgrim swore those wild eyes were following him as he moved around the room but wrote it off to those circulating mists. On each side of the Founder were two other sarcophagi containing his predecessors—their eternal resting places were covered, unlike the Founder's.

Maybe I'll have them replace the Founder's body with my own. Who would know the difference?

Blasphemy! Am I going mad? It occurred to him the Founder could have gone mad too. *Another blasphemy!* He fell to his knees, laid his forehead against the cold stone, and prayed, but sleep took him after an hour in that pious position.

The next morning a messenger told him about the attacks on New Hope and Long Beach.

Chapter Thirty-Three

A Good Day to Live

Tristan put down his tablet and looked up as Kaushal entered his hovel. Both men were dressed in armor and carried their usual weapons.

Kaushal studied his mentor, a teacher of the skills of war as well as the strange philosophy of the Way. In some sense, Tristan was a younger Pel—both wise men who weren't afraid of a fight. *How old were they? If someday I take those longevity drugs, will I still be able to do battle as they do?*

Kaushal saw Tristan's tablet was full of strange symbols. "What are you calculating, old friend?"

"Our chances." Tristan tapped the tablet. "One can apply the theory of social dynamics even to smaller planetary populations. The error bars are much larger, of course, so large I can only make a few general conclusions about our weak spots. We're better off than before, though."

"I suppose marching on Angels' Bay is one of those weak spots." Kaushal figured a direct attack at the seat of the theocracy's power was always ill-advised. When the beast is cornered, it becomes desperate and fights with abandon.

"Not so much as last time. Surprises can occur, of course. No, the calculations show most of our weakness comes from not knowing how many First Tribesmen will throw in with us as we move on the castle. The local population is dominated by First Tribesmen. We're better than before, like I said. Our propaganda efforts have enlightened many and given hope to many who had lost it." He smiled. "I believe we're past the tipping point, and the theocracy will fall. The calculations still say the outcome is unknown, though." He put the tablet down. "Do you have information for me?"

"Kindri reported New Hope fell and Long Beach is going well. The king's soldiers in those cities are no longer motivated to fight, and the public isn't in the mood to maintain their supply chains. They're not Angels' Bay, of course, but the propaganda campaign had to help there too."

Tristan nodded. "Good. Are you ready?"

"Pel, Kiana, and I made a trial run yesterday evening. We parked in that glen down the mountain."

"It's doable then?" said Tristan.

"With difficulty. A question arises: in which group should I go?" He fell into a lotus position in front of Tristan. "You know the palace. You should be in one group, I in another."

"We discussed that. There's no guarantee of success. Someone has to be here to pick up the pieces if things don't work out. I have the big picture, more so than Kiana and Pel."

"Choose Kifi or Ezan for that. They don't know the castle. Or Pel. We need Kiana, but he's not needed."

"Kiana needs backup. Pel serves that function for her and for you, so that's settled." Tristan thought a moment. "But your question is valid. Who will reach the First Pilgrim first?"

"It depends on how he distributes his bodyguards, and their willingness to defend the old bastard. I'm guessing the group not scaling the seawall, but—" Kaushal indicated the tablet. "—I have none of your fancy symbols and equations that allow me to predict that."

"My equations can't predict that outcome either, but you should be in that group if you have that gut feeling. And that group will be in the most danger, so the other will be backup. Remember, Kaushal, the people need a king. Never forget that."

"Until they learn they don't," said Kaushal. "You can make someone else king if I perish. I'm prepared to die. I no longer fear the Almighty Ra. The Way has taught me to accept what comes to me."

"You still have a lot to learn about the Way. Pel once lost it, but returned to it. It's not easy to follow the Way. Humans are unreasonable, illogical, and emotional; logic and reason don't come easily to them."

"Logic and reason tell me the outcome of a battle can be subject to chance, in spite of your fancy analysis. Opponents' actions aren't predictable. How can I not accept the possibility I might perish? I have no magical powers."

"Sometimes you have to make your own magic. I'm not saying it's impossible you'll perish. I'm saying your responsibility is to prevent it if at all possible. Let's suppose the First Pilgrim flees. Will you pursue?" Kaushal nodded. "No! He might be leading you into a trap. That old shakma is a devious monster. He might be evil, but he's not dumb. He'll be prepared. And you'll be cornering the shakma in his den."

"We might not have another chance," said Kaushal.

"We will. We can always plot again, as many times as needed. No despotic regime lasts forever."

***

Kindri raised his hand. Arrows flew into the garrison, their tips soaked in lamp oil already flaming, a primitive but effective way to soften the enemy. He watched for the reaction.

They'd known Long Beach wouldn't be as easy as New Hope. It would become more difficult nearer Angels' Bay.

The street battles in Long Beach had taken two days. Now only the garrison was left.

Samos was already a casualty in the street fighting. He had drawn the short straw to lead the advance through the town, a difficult one because the port city's defenders knew those narrow streets better than rebel troops. Although frightened citizens hid from both sides, it didn't take many soldiers with their superior knowledge of the geography to do a lot of damage. Samos and others had been led into traps throughout the city. Fighting was still going on, but troops defending the city would succumb to the rebel onslaught, even with losses.

Through his binoculars, Kindri could see the rain of arrows was sowing confusion among the garrison's defenders. It would soon be time to lead the charge. Many more would fall, and those in the garrison would perish if they didn't surrender.

At his belt were two pistols and something called a taser. Across his back was an automatic rifle. But he also had a long knife and scimitar. Their weapons were an unusual mix, their supply augmented by the fall of New Hope when soldiers there surrendered without much fight. But he hesitated. *Who knows what this garrison has?* He could imagine cannons and flame throwers and other weapons making the siege last.

In a quiet moment, he heard the beep of his tablet. He reached behind and took it from his backpack.

The message from Tristan read: *Give them a chance to surrender.*

No way! he thought. *Who knows what atrocities these soldiers have committed?* But they had surrendered at New Hope after rebels took control of the city. *Isn't that the situation here?*

He smiled. He had a solution. Maybe he could avoid heavy casualties on both sides. *Chance is subject to interpretation, Tristan.* He passed the word: another rain of arrows, this time with messages.

It appeared his plan had worked. After a few moments, the garrison gate opened and a lone figure emerged, holding a white flag. He sent a return message back to Tristan: *Looks like they want to talk. I'm going down.*

They constructed a flag for him from a pike and a warrior's white shirt. Kindri left his weapons behind and marched down the hill and over the berm to the approaching figure, who stopped, planted his flag, and clicked his boots in salute. The soldier was also unarmed. Just in case, Kindri had the pike with his makeshift flag.

"Major-General Marco Watney, leader of this garrison." The usual fist-to-heart salute. Kindri noticed the loving hands of the Almighty Ra cradling the world on the fellow's tunic were bloodied. "Your rank and name, sir?"

Hmm, we have no ranks in this rebel army. It was a diverse mix of Mountain Folk, Wilders, and fed-up people, both First and Second Tribesmen, from the cities. So Kindri made up a rank.

"Commander Kindri, leader of the Wilders' Expeditionary Force, troops in the service of King Kaushal."

Marco smiled. "That sounds about as truthful as saying jonkis can fly." He shrugged and offered a hand. "Never mind. I'm here to negotiate our surrender."

Kindri shook it. "Are your troops prepared to atone for their sins?"

"Are you kidding? What's that mean?"

"I don't know. It sounded good." It was Kindri's turn to smile. "Maybe admit to killing and maiming the citizens of Long Beach?"

"I've never done that. We're stationed here to preserve order and protect those citizens from barbarians like you."

"So why surrender? The First Pilgrim would want you to battle to the end."

"The First Pilgrim is a dirty old man who blasphemes the Founder and the Almighty Ra. We'll die for the latter, but not for the First Pilgrim. Understood?"

"And swear allegiance to King Kaushal?"

"Whatever. I've never met him. It's hard to imagine he'd be worse than the First Pilgrim, though, or that hedonistic lout, King Farben. What are your terms, Commander Kindri?"

They came to an agreement. An hour later, Marco's men filed from the garrison after releasing their prisoners. The latter and a small contingent Kindri left behind would maintain peace in Long Beach. The majority of the force would now move on toward Angels' Bay.

Kindri would remember Marco Watney, though. The man was a survivor and intelligent.

***

When the battle for Angels' Bay started four days later, it looked a lot like the first one, except this time there were fewer Royal Guards and other troops, and they received no help from the population, except for the few remaining spies and turncoats in service to the First Pilgrim. What the enemy lacked in numbers, though, was compensated for by their superior weapons and communications again. They soon came to a standoff with opposing forces facing each other across Angels' River.

"Each side knows they'll take huge losses if they cross the river and attack the other," said Tristan. "I didn't see this coming."

220

"Never mind, old friend," said Kaushal buckling on the final pieces of his armor. "Your equations couldn't have foreseen this. They've dug in. You'll figure out something. We can't stare at each other forever. And we're ready to move, so it might not matter. Wish us luck."

"Not luck. Skill. I wish all of you skill in battle. I'm afraid you'll need it. The castle is more fortified than ever. Talk about digging in!"

Kaushal noted the man's weapons. "And where are you going?"

"A few others and I are taking the Golden Scimitar to a safe place. We'll protect it. It's now your symbol of authority, you know, not Kovlyn's."

Kaushal laughed. "It's a good weapon, but that's all it is. I'm not taking it; it's too heavy. I discovered that when Anju and I dispatched those soldiers in front of Chobi's pub."

"I wouldn't have let you take it. It can at least be used to make Anju Eden's queen."

"She already is, at least in spirit. If I'm king, she's my queen. But she values the Scimitar as little as I do."

"It's the underpinning for your entire culture," said Tristan. "Humans often need such icons, although I'll never understand why. Your history is full of icons and statues and places of worship. Some historian will have to make sense of it all someday."

Kaushal studied Tristan. The old man said strange things sometimes. Kaushal had seen no evidence for such a need on New Haven. He hoped he'd see the day when Eden was like that.

"We'll discuss this later," said Kaushal. "We'd best be on our way."

"As you wish, my king," said Tristan with a slight smile and bow.

Chapter Thirty-Four

Kovlyn Organizes

General Ynesh entered the First Pilgrim's study, gave the usual fist-to-heart salute, and bowed. His uniform had multiple medals, and his purple cape carried the gold insignia of the First Tribe, cupped hands holding a planet, a bit more ornate than the average soldier's. That planet in the symbol had first been an iconic Paradise; now it was Eden. He rose and followed the correct protocol of waiting for the Almighty Ra's representative on Eden to speak. The general's spit and polish were impeccable but not extravagant beyond the tunic. He was a fighting man, not a pompous member of the nobility.

Kovlyn eyed his general long enough to make the latter twitch. *Fools still fear the King's Mage!* He decided he could always rule by fear although their respect was gone. Given time, the respect would return. *Or else!*

"I hope you have good news," he said.

Ynesh licked his lips and twitched some more. "We have stopped their advance. We assume we have the upper hand now."

"'We assume'? Do you have it or not? I want a leader who knows. Guesses, not even educated ones, don't make the grade with me." Kovlyn's fist slammed on the desk. Ynesh jumped. "Do I need to replace you?"

"No, sir. We think—I know we have an attack plan that will rout the rebels. They are trapped between the river and ocean with our troops on the river's opposite side. We can send a flotilla of troop carriers around the coast and march across flood plains to attack their rear. They will be crushed between our two forces."

Kovlyn nodded. "That sounds reasonable. What's stopping you?"

"The number of troops. I'm afraid their spies will see we're spread too thin between the river and castle and tell other rebels to attack, hoping to win the castle."

Kovlyn jerked. "That can't happen! Never! The castle has to be defended at all cost. It is hallowed ground and always has been. And who are these spies?"

"Ordinary citizens mostly, who have turned against us. We've captured a few, but there are many of them."

"Good. Torture the ones you captured. Determine who their families are. Kill them all!"

"They have all resisted and died before divulging any useful intel, sir. They are well trained. And it's difficult to root them out. They look like everyone else."

Kovlyn detected admiration in the man's voice. *Am I losing my most trusted general?* "Move the flotilla at night. The trip's not that long. Attack the rebel forces at dawn."

"Sailing at night is difficult," said Ynesh, "and there are reefs right below the waterline at high tides. The admiral doesn't want to risk it."

"Replace him with someone who does then, you stupid jonki! We're done here."

"Yes, sir." Ynesh bowed and backed out.

***

At midnight, loyalist troops filed onto the huge ships. With the weight of soldiers and equipment, the ships sat low in the water. General Ynesh was no sailor, but he worried about that. But he figured he'd need every one of them and all the equipment if his armies were going to rout the rebel forces. Morale was low too. He had already seen it was high among the rebels. He stared at the inky waters and said a silent prayer to the Almighty Ra. He turned and went inside.

He was a guest on Admiral Sanjay's ship. He joined the corpulent man at the table reserved for Navy officers. The fat fool wouldn't have much to do on this voyage beyond providing transportation.

Still, Ynesh liked Sanjay. One day he hoped to marry his daughter who looked more like her mother and not Sanjay. He had none of his five wives with him. *At least he's smart enough to realize this mission is dangerous!* He knew Sanjay had often taken his wives with him when the fleet attacked Wilders in the Southlands. His orgies before and after battles were already legend.

He offered a toast to the admiral as he sensed the ship had set sail, old motors wheezing and yet still needing aid from sails. *If I survive this, I'm going to use my prestige to make the First Pilgrim overhaul this whole fleet. It's a disgrace!*

"This isn't going to be easy," said Sanjay making a bad face at the sour wine and spitting it out. "You know, because of the southern campaigns, I haven't had a decent drink in months. These rebels must be vanquished so we can return to our normal lives and reacquire our trade routes."

"Where is your difficulty?" said Ynesh, forgetting about the wine. "My forces have to attack and win a bloody battle. Your sailors only have to take us around the coast."

Sanjay frowned. "If a ship hits a reef, your forces will know what difficulty is. It would be easier if you allowed us some running lights. We're like a blind man in a dark cave feeling his way around."

"With lights, we might as well put out a sign saying, 'We're attacking you from the rear.' Besides, if one or two of your ships goes down, we're still ensured success. We outnumber the rebels. You'll be able to pound your chest—

watching for all those medals, of course—and boast of our exploits."

"But who is protecting the castle?"

Ynesh shrugged. "A problem, old friend. Rebels will figure out our strategy soon enough, I fear, but it will be too late for them to do anything about it. Do you have any biscuits? I can't go into battle on an empty stomach. And I need to dull this taste of bad wine."

***

The admiral lost none of his ships, but two landing skiffs carrying twenty men each floundered on hidden rocks. Some drowned from the weight of their heavy armor. Others managed to strip it off. They were picked up by other boats.

Ynesh and his forces landed. The beach had a steep grade until it leveled where they could reassemble to check armor and weapons. They also rested a bit. Moving uphill in the sand with heavy armor had tired even powerful legs.

The general surveyed his ranks of soldiers and liked what he saw. With about nine hundred men, he wasn't sure they outnumbered the rebels, but, as always, they were better equipped and better trained.

He smiled. It was ironic old Second Tribe technology would be used against a rebel group mostly composed of Second Tribesmen. His father had told him stories about how the First Tribe had come as refugees to Eden with very little. He had to give it to the old First Pilgrim. He was a schemer even if he was such a pervert. Ynesh still wasn't sure he wanted to die for the man, though.

Admiral Sanjay and his flotilla went farther offshore and dropped anchor to wait. It wasn't an escape route for Ynesh and his men, though. Their route would be through rebel forces and then back toward the castle. Sanjay just wanted to return to port by daylight. *The man wants to live a hundred years!* Of course, his daughter was something else. She would be a great trophy after Ynesh defeated the rebels. And with the fame he achieved with the victory, the old fart couldn't deny him.

"We are ready, general," said one of his officers, giving the fist-to-heart salute of the loyalist forces. "What are your orders, sir?"

"They haven't changed. Stealth. I'll kill the man who allows a sword to clank or a gun to accidentally fire. Absolute silence until we're in position." He raised his message tablet. "Have these handy along the lines. When I give the word, attack. Show no mercy. Don't leave wounded. Kill them so they can't fight another day. That will also save us the bother of executing and burying the fools."

"Yes, sir." The soldier spun and left to return to his platoon.

The timing couldn't have been better. The purple skies of dawn in the east provided the promise of day when Ynesh stood on top of one hill overlooking the rebel encampment along the river. After a few minutes of looking each way along his rows of soldiers, he lowered his helmet visor, took his tablet, and sent the message. *Attack!*

Chapter Thirty-Five

The Encampment

The loyalists used the same trick rebels employed at the Long Beach garrison. A rain of flaming arrows fell on the rebels' bivouac tents. That rude wakeup call resulted in some rebels leaving armor and weapons behind as they fled the flames. Kindri had the presence of mind to scoop up all his weapons and armor, though. So did Kifi and Ezan, as well as other more seasoned troops.

Kifi pointed to the rolling hills between them and the sea. "They're coming from the hills behind us! We'll be trapped with our backs to the river. We must move forward and take the initiative."

"You heard the woman!" said Kindri. "Archers and snipers move left and right and do as much damage as you can shooting along their advancing lines. Everyone else push forward." He raised his scimitar and one pistol, a taser still tucked in his belt. They had used their last stolen batteries to charge the few they had. "It's a good day to die!"

"Not before I kill some of Kovlyn's soldiers," said Ezan. She assumed a marksman's stance, steadied, and fired her pistol twice. Two advancing loyalists in the distance went down. Kindri was surprised. Even with one eye, she still had a lethal aim. "For King Kaushal!"

The rebel lines moved forward. The two groups met, and the furious battle comprised mostly of hand-to-hand fighting ensued. Rebel archers and snipers started pruning loyalist ranks from the ends. Even with their primitive weapons, their aim was still deadly. The rebels were more motivated; the loyalists lethargic. Most of the latter spoke the First Tribe's dialect; the ones who didn't surrendered, joined rebel forces, or ran toward the sea.

***

The battle raged for more than a standard hour. It became a throwback to ancient times as ammo for older weapons disappeared and newer ones lost their charge. Kindri knocked out one opponent with his discharged taser by throwing the heavy weapon at the loyalist. Broadswords, scimitars, pikes, and long knives clashed against armor and through flesh, and rebel and loyalist arrows alike came down like monsoon torrents from the sky.

As Eden's sun warmed the battlefield, dense fog also blew in from the ocean, making the lush hills damp and eerie while muting the sounds of battle. They were like ghosts battling over the souls of the fallen. As broadswords were swung, heavy boots searching for purchase turned the hills' fertile soil into cloying mud. More than one slip ended in death for a combatant.

When their general fell victim to Kifi's sword, her final mortal blow was stopped by his "We surrender!"

She hoisted him up. "Tell the rest of your men!"

He nodded. "I'm taking out my message tablet. Only platoon leaders have one, although they might be dead by now. Be patient, witch!"

She laughed, placing her sword's edge to his throat. "Be careful, Ynesh, or I will put a hex on you. It might be worse than death. But send your message now or die!"

***

"They must have reduced numbers across the river now," said Kindri, adjusting the bandage on his arm. He was studying the opposite side with his binoculars.

She hadn't had time to work her magic and stitch him up. Besides, she had neither the antiseptic liquor nor the surgical thread. The bandage had been torn from her blouse. She put her armor back on. Other rebels were tending to comrades. They had lost many on the battlefield, but the complaints of the wounded and dying left her numb.

"If we go toward the tidal flats and wade across, we can send troops right toward the castle and left to those who remain in the loyalist encampment," said Kifi. "What do you think?"

"Let's do it," said Ezan, not waiting for Kindri's opinion.

Kindri lowered the binoculars and thought a moment. "We don't have enough troops to guard the prisoners," he said. "The healthy ones can still attack us, including that old scoundrel, General Ynesh."

"Maybe not troops," said Kifi, pointing.

Old men, women, and children were pouring from the village, the first one upriver from the capital. The younger men from there were probably fighting on one side or the other.

"Can we trust them?" said Kindri. As a Wilder who spoke a combination of the First and Second Tribe's dialects, he had a hard time deciphering what the people running toward them were yelling.

Kifi watched, listened, and smiled. There were only the cheers of a happy people.

"They're jubilant about our win," said Ezan. "We'll have to give explicit instructions so they won't harm the prisoners. These same people likely had relatives who were tortured and executed, and these same loyalists might have paraded around with their heads on pikes. It's hard to forgive something like that. Kifi can talk to them." She put her hand on the Wilder's shoulder. "You and I and other leaders must organize our march across the river. The route will be clearer now but still not easy."

Kifi and Kindri nodded their agreement.

***

They stared across the river waters, still dark in the weak light of morning and hidden by fog and mist still stretching from the opposite side to the sea. Vapors from the river added to that reduced visibility.

A loyalist soldier broke loose from his two captors, stepped forward, and called to them.

"I know what you're considering! There's quicksand in the tidal flats. At high tide, right below the surface. What looks like sure footing is a deathtrap."

Kindri studied the old man for a bit and then beckoned him to come forward. "Your name, soldier."

He snapped to attention, giving the fist-to-heart salute of loyalists. "Lakus Jenti, my liege. Once a fisherman, now a soldier. I lived in that village. We're unwilling conscripts in the loyalist army."

"You'd better forget that salute if you don't want to die a slow death then," said Kindri with a smile. "We don't stand on ceremony like that. And thank you for your advice." He clasped the shoulder of the fisherman. "Are you companions with us now?"

"We never were with them. We had to fight or our families would either die or starve, which is the same thing, of course. To whom do we swear allegiance?"

"To Prince Kaushal, son of King Merson, soon to be future king of Eden."

Lakus smiled. "That explains a lot of recent events, I suppose. I speak for the other villagers. The prince now has our complete loyalty."

"That's good news. Your warning is not, though. Do you know a safe route across the flats?"

The ex-loyalist looked at the sky with only a hint of a sun and shook his head. "When I was a boy, I knew a way. The currents of the tributary are changeable, though. The river swells with the snow melt from the mountain peaks every spring and new channels and deathtraps are formed. Let me find my oldest son. He's the one who fishes in the flats now. My life is more at sea. Or was. It's a good idea to go across the flats, though. What man thought of it? I commend him."

Kindri now laughed. "No man, Lakus. The idea came from a woman named Kifi, the one who captured the loyalists' general."

"Oh, my. He'll never live that one down. Unless she ended his miserable life to avoid the embarrassment."

"Your village brothers and sisters will keep him safe," said Kindri, "and possibly have some fun mocking him, poor man. Help me find your boy."

In ten minutes, the son, who looked to be about fifteen, stood before Kindri, shifting his feet and looking from his father to Kindri. His name was Talfri. He was nearly as tall as his father. The group of soldiers made him nervous. He was unarmed and nearly naked, dressed only in a short, rough kilt with the weave and faded colors characteristic of the village.

Lakus nodded to him. "These people want some help getting across the river in the shallows."

"You'll be exposed," the boy said, "because the route I know requires you to go single file. There's no other route. I can lead the way, but we'll be dancing around quicksand traps. And we can't wait 'til evening because I need to see the opposite shore for reference."

"We can have snipers and bowmen bring up the rear," said Kifi, who'd joined the group after turning the captured soldiers over to the villagers. "How long will it take to cross?"

"Even at low tide, the current is strong, and out to sea," said Lakus. "You have to walk gingerly as if you were heading upriver a little. But not too much."

"One stumble and you can fall into quicksand," said Talfri. "Let's say we're moving half a kilometer per standard hour toward the opposite shore. The river is about a kilometer wide where we'll be crossing. You can do the math."

Kindri smiled. The kid was sharp and had a young man's ego. "Two hours or longer then."

"We have to hazard it," said Kifi. "Going upriver to the bridge across the narrows would take too long. And our two-pronged attack won't work then."

"How far is that?" said Kindri.

"Past the village, maybe five kilometers," said Lakus.

"Any chance we can go in twos or threes?" said Kifi.

"Not unless you ride on my shoulders," said Talfri with a smile.

"In your dreams, boy," said Kifi.

"Now that's an idea, though," said Kindri. "If ten men with women on their shoulders cross first, that's a respectable advance guard."

"You're serious?" said Ezan. "Think about it. If my guy steps in quicksand, we'll sink a lot faster because the two of us weigh more than one."

Kifi shrugged. "I'm not going on a diet, so I guess we'd better ensure our guys don't step in the muck. I'm game. Let's do it."

Chapter Thirty-Six

The Attack on Starlight Castle

Group A would need more time to reach the seawall and rappel to the small window, where they would enter one by one. Group B, Kaushal's group, waited in the mountains for word from A that they had arrived before they moved out. If things went right, the commandoes would enter Starlight Castle at the same time.

Group B was smaller, but Kiana's stolen spaceship *Mosca* was still crowded. The added weight made it more difficult to control as they skimmed over mountain peaks and descended toward Angels' Bay. Flying low minimized chances they would be seen too soon, but it tested Kiana's skills as a pilot.

Pel put a hand on his wife's shoulder. She took a second to smile at him. "I have this under control. We had our practice run. Brace yourselves. I'm going to increase altitude only enough to come in low over the castle complex."

Some members of the group gasped. They had never experienced an elevator—the only ones in existence on Eden were in the castle—let alone the flight of such a vehicle. Things began to shake and wobble too as it descended to hover over one of the battlements.

"Be nimble," she said. "I don't know how long I can hold this."

"Sit it down," said Pel.

"Not enough room," said his wife. "We'll topple over the side. Get your ass in gear, old man, or we're going to crash!"

Kaushal was the first one to slide down the rope, though, and Pel was the last. He glanced upward as Kiana took off, waving to her. He turned to Kaushal.

"Lead the way, prince. We have your back."

"Then follow me, old man," said Kaushal with a grin. He approached a wall that had an inset area. He reached up, found a switch, and that portion slid open to reveal an entranceway. He enjoyed seeing Pel's expression. "My father was a sly old fox. No one knows about these secret doors and passageways but me now, but they were part of my playground as a child."

They followed him inside. As they moved through corridors and stairways, lights flared ahead of them and dimmed behind as usual, but Kaushal noticed that some illumination was missing now—nothing lasted forever. In those dimly lit spots, he moved with care. After a bit, they turned a corner into a brighter corridor, and Kaushal raised his hand.

"That was easy," he said. "Now comes the hard part." He put his ear against the wall.

"Easy, lad," said Pel, putting a hand on Kaushal's shoulder. "Let the Way guide your actions."

Kaushal reached up and another panel slid open.

***

Kiana had picked her landing spot from a map. She wished she had access to real-time satellite data from the ITUIP explorer ship in orbit above, though, when she saw what was waiting for her. *Damn the Protocol!*

The group of Palace Guards, most likely lowly, off-duty castle sentries, were having a bit of fun with some women.

She couldn't tell if they were castle staff or whores from the city, but the soldiers were slapping and pawing at them. They showed no interest in the nearby fighting in the city. *Drunken louts! Oh well…here goes!*

Kaushal had invented the decoration on the ship's undercarriage, and they had all worked to paint it on. A representation of the Devil's image, the prince had remembered it from an old castle mural. The Evil One's huge hands, more like talons, were raised alongside the face as if he were ready to grab any unwitting souls beneath him. Kiana had protested about defacing their ship with religious symbolism, but now she knew it would come in handy. *Superstition is a powerful weapon!*

What little noise the ship made upon landing was lost in the laughing drunks' guffaws and their intended victims' lusty screeches. Only when the huge shadow fell on the group did they look skyward and discover what was descending upon them. Both drunks and women wasted no time in fleeing, fright etched on all their faces.

As she landed, Kiana was still laughing at the sight of seasoned soldiers, many naked from the waist down, and women, many still holding skirts above their waists, dashing off to seek refuge from the Devil. *Kaushal, you are a genius!*

For the moment, she was safe. Her thoughts turned to the groups inside the castle, especially Group B. Pel was still her husband, but that didn't stop Kiana from loving Kaushal. Her love for Pel had matured with the centuries—her time away from him had always made her feel she was missing the most important person in her life. Kaushal had been only an assignment at first, a stealth mission, but she had grown to love the young man too. *The longer I live, the more room for love,* she thought. She knew if Kaushal lived through this, he would be serving his people afterward. She had Pel; she worried about Anju. The Way never allowed anyone to predict the future. They would have to wait and see how it all played out.

She stretched back in her pilot's seat and decided to take a snooze.

Whatever the outcome was, she and Pel would move on. Their lives now only had meaning in their continued efforts to help the downtrodden. Every decade and every century brought new adventures. That meant losing old friends and gaining new ones. She'd have it no other way. *Well, maybe not the losses.*

***

The eunuchs, most of them Second Tribesmen, had no weapons. Even those who were First Tribesmen took in the situation and stepped aside, not out of fear, but motioning the castle's invaders along without resistance, some smiling.

The Palace Guards were another question. Some fought to the death. The commandoes had guns, but they didn't use them much in close quarters. Kaushal was an exception because he led the group. Sword in one hand, pistol in the other, he and the others fought their way through groups of Guards. Sometimes when they heard the clang of armor from other approaching groups, Kaushal would lead them into another secret corridor. In and out, hit and run. It was a useful tactic, one Group A could also use because they carried Kaushal's diagrams, but their progress would be slower—Kaushal didn't need to refer to maps.

Pel surprised Kaushal; he took his swordsmanship to another level. He would take on two or three enemy combatants at a time, grunting and yelling with the best of them. He used his flowing robe to confuse them or to sneak in a thrust. Twice he saved Kaushal. Kaushal saved him once too, and two other castle invaders.

"This way!"

A panel opened, and once again the group moved into a dimly lit corridor.

"Yet another secret passageway?" said Pel. "Your father was a crazy man!"

"Let's hope the first group has entered via the seawall and is making similar progress. This time they'll be scaling the castle wall right next to the First Pilgrim's balcony."

"Is he likely to be there?" said another commando.

"Even if he is, he'll be looking at the city and the river from a greater height than Group A's entry point to where the major fighting is going on. I'm counting on that." Kaushal rubbed his hand on the granite. "Anju and I used this route when we stole the Scimitar, so we'll soon know whether Kovlyn is in his quarters."

He wasn't. As Kaushal had predicted, they saw him on the balcony, eating dinner and watching the distant battle on the castle's side of the river. He must have just arrived and drawn the heavy curtains, their draw cords still swinging. Bad and good luck! Bad, because Group A was fighting elsewhere and hadn't captured him. Good, because he hadn't seen the other group scaling the wall. Group A had moved through beneath him. Success now depended on Kaushal's Group B.

Is he worried? The Founder's anointed seemed to be savoring his dinner. *Will it be his last?*

Kaushal wondered how the battle by the river was going. *It doesn't matter right now.* He turned to his men and put a finger to his lips.

The remainder of the group crowded behind him as he approached the old man's back. *One sweep of my sword will end this despot!* Kaushal thought.

Instead he said, "You're no longer fit to be this king's First Pilgrim or his Mage."

Kovlyn jumped up and faced him. "You! The master singer. I should have known. I thought I recognized you. You're Prince Kaushal!"

"My whole life. And I've spent all of it despising you and everything you stand for!"

The priest drew his sword and rushed Kaushal. With his party behind him, the prince had nowhere to go. He parried the powerful thrust; sparks flew. Others started to make room and soon became busy as Palace Guards poured into the room behind them. Kaushal knew why: he saw the call-box hanging from Kovlyn's neck. Technology made the Mage's magic real; superstition made it powerful.

In spite of his age, the First Pilgrim fought like a young warrior. Several times his sword came within a centimeter of Kaushal as the Mage pressed the attack. But Kaushal fought back. The design of the Almighty Ra's hands holding Eden on the back of that royal purple robe soon showed streaks of bright red. But the fury in the priest's eyes didn't abate. He seemed to acquire strength from his desperation. This was no lethargic, loyalist soldier who had no real desire to fight for the First Pilgrim. *He's a man possessed who believes the Almighty Ra gives him the strength to overcome his opponents.*

There was a step down from the study onto that balcony. As Kaushal backed up, he tripped on its edge. His sword went flying. As the old man wound up for a mortal blow, both hands on the sword, Kaushal shot him.

Kovlyn staggered backward, stopped, and then flashed a wicked grin.

Armor! Under that robe, the First Pilgrim must be wearing bullet-proof armor. *I should have cut off his head!*

The First Pilgrim advanced again, this time with more caution but still with confidence. He probably realized the next time Kaushal would aim for his head. Kaushal tried, but he heard the empty click and realized he no longer had any rounds chambered. He had used them all in the earlier confrontations, leaving him helpless now.

"Your group's members are either dead or incapacitated," said Kovlyn. "Give it up and I promise you a merciful death."

"One of your beheading spectacles, I suppose" said Kaushal, standing and lowering the gun. He unsheathed his dagger and held it to his throat. "I prefer to die right here."

"No," said a voice behind Kaushal. A hirsute arm pulled his knife hand away.

"Good," said the First Pilgrim. "Arrest him and throw him in chains! I take back what I said. I will have some entertaining hours planning a worse death for this jonki whelp of a Second Tribe King."

"I'm afraid the chains are for you, Kovlyn," said Ravik.

***

Palace Guards under Ravik's command were loyal to him, not Kovlyn. That meant they were loyal to Kaushal. They and Kaushal's Group B commandoes had made short work of the other Palace Guards, but Kovlyn had thought they were all his own men.

They didn't have chains, but they bound the First Pilgrim in the purple draw cords taken from the heavy curtains. They didn't worry about how tight they were either. The First Pilgrim grimaced in pain.

"Your other group is securing the castle," Ravik said to Kaushal, Pel, and the others. "My men will help. Can you and Pel keep this pile of drax excrement under guard?"

"With pleasure," said Pel. He offered a chair to Kovlyn. "Have a seat, your holiness, so we can discuss your punishment calmly. I assure you we won't take hours doing it. We'll allow your input, of course. You have enough experience in doling it out, so I expect you to be creative."

"I too can suggest many possibilities," said Kaushal.

"I bet you can," Pel said to him. "Follow the Way, Prince Kaushal. Are your possibilities commensurate with what you have learned?"

Kaushal hung his head. "No. Doing to him what he has done to others is too simple. What should we do?"

"What do you suggest, your holiness?" Pel said to Kovlyn.

The First Pilgrim glared at them. "Are you kidding me?" He stared at the balcony and glared again at them. "I expect no mercy, and I'll be the martyr who ascends into the loving arms of the Almighty Ra. I'll embrace Osiris and kiss Isis. I have no idea what this Way is you're talking about, but it sounds like blasphemy."

Pel sighed. "Not enough people do. But it's an old tradition. When Humans first explored their home solar system, a new philosophy appropriate to the long hauls between planets was needed. Guides to the Way stole a bit from many religions, you see, but it's more a philosophical acceptance of our oneness with the Universe."

"As I said, that sounds like heresy," said Kovlyn, eyeing the balcony again.

At that moment, Kiana entered. Pel stood and hugged her.

Kaushal smiled, but not for long. The First Pilgrim, taking advantage of the distraction, ran to the balcony and jumped.

"Not on my list of suggestions," said Kaushal, going to the balcony's bannister and looking down at the smashed body floating in the roiling waters swirling around the rocks below. "But it works."

Pel peered over his shoulder. "Martyrdom becomes him," he said.

Chapter Thirty-Seven

The Reunion

"I guess it's over," said Kifi. "All but the clean-up." She had left her armor and weapons on a pile in one corner of the room and had only a kilt on. She looked weary but relaxed. In spite of streaks of blood, soil, and sweat on her face and torso, Kaushal thought she still looked beautiful.

"Be merciful," he said.

Pel nodded. He had joined Kifi and the crowd of disrobing members of Groups A and B and other rebel leaders who had come to the palace. Their actions reinforced Kifi's first statement. They were symbolic too—Starlight Castle now belonged to the rebels.

"We'll have to watch for those who are reluctant to accept the coming changes," said Pel, "but the better we treat people, the better chance they will accept."

"That's wise," said Kindri.

He had left his boots on and rested his feet on the heavy wooden table while tilting back his ornately carved chair. They were in the huge dining room where Kaushal had once sung for King Breman. Kaushal didn't have the heart to tell Kindri to take his feet down. They were all exhausted.

"I gave Lakus, his boy, and some others the chore of guarding our little ship," said Kiana. She fingered the pendant on a necklace that hung in the cleavage of her perky breasts. Kaushal hadn't seen it before, but it looked foreign. It was black with a gold filigree featuring a regular V, a carpenter's square, intertwined with a vertical one, a compass. *Did she stash it in the Mosca when we fled Quick Death?* He winked at her.

She had flown the little ship with an expert's touch. "It might be the only functional one we have left. Those two villagers came highly recommended by Kifi and Kindri."

"Tristan and some others are descending from the mountains with the Scimitar," said Pel. He smiled at Kaushal. "It's time for you to become the official king."

Kaushal frowned. *I only need to be with Anju.*

Rivak and his men found a barrel of the finest wine and tapped it. A party began. After some rounds, many laudatory comments tending toward bragging were offered, as well as many toasts. Kaushal soon became pensive and left the party early.

***

Kaushal wandered Starlight Castle. It would soon be his castle if he wanted it. *Will it be a good home for Anju and me?* He didn't know what home meant anymore, but he'd spent more years in the castle than anywhere else, good times when progressive thought and logic and reason seemed to permeate the air. While evil was dissipating now, they would have to work hard to make it a home again.

He no longer needed the secret doors and passageways. That time was gone, more a part of his childhood than anything else. But he had decided it was simpler to leave them. Other children could always use them, turning the whole castle into a playground like he had.

He visited the garden where he had fallen in love with Anju. He also visited the magic room, still full of electronic junk and still showing the huge, dark screens. *Had the ITUIP's surveillance ship discovered the video channels and shut them down?*

He shrugged. It didn't matter. He would forever remember the wonders of New Haven and near-space. That had been so much more real than the blurry images of those who enforced the quarantine and watched how events unfolded on the surface. *But is my future here on Eden or out there?*

"I thought I might find you here," said Tristan.

Kaushal turned and faced him. He was standing in the doorway, smiling at his protégé.

He strode forward and handed Kaushal the Golden Scimitar.

"You can take care of this now," he said. "In a few days, Kiana, Pel, and I will be leaving." He waved at the wall screens. "Our work here is done. We'll have to go back to New Haven and receive our punishment."

"Punishment? Why would they punish you?"

"For breaking the rules, although the Protocol doesn't specify the type of punishment when they're violated. I guess they didn't want to make it specific so they can adapt to different situations. But don't worry. Kiana and Pel are accustomed to these things."

"And you?"

Tristan smiled. "We'll see. Punishment isn't the only ambiguity in the Protocol." He watched Kaushal hook the Scimitar onto his wide belt. "It's heavy, isn't it? The responsibility that goes with it is heavy too."

"Yes, the weight of being Eden's ruler. Kovlyn didn't trust First Tribe kings with it, but I'm not sure I trust myself either. I'm not ready. I might never be ready."

"Don't worry about that either. Shall we return to the celebration? They'll be missing you." Tristan hooked his arm into Kaushal's. "You can lead the way. My memory functions are a bit slow these days."

"Were you already drinking?"

"No, just old age. Human beings used to call it senility. In space—" he waved a hand toward the ceiling "—we call it a need for a tune-up."

***

As they walked back through the castle, Kaushal noticed the signs of battle in many areas. Most bodies had been removed, but weapons and scents of blood, urine, and feces still hung in the air. *How many people died here today? For that matter, how many deaths did the First Pilgrim and his sycophants cause in their reign of terror?* Many years of bloodshed had now ended. Would there now be many years of peace and prosperity? King or not, he knew he had to ensure that. He could never leave Eden otherwise.

Tristan was silent with his own thoughts. Kaushal couldn't understand the need for punishment. Kiana, Pel, and Tristan had worked to overthrow the First Pilgrim and his despotic theocracy. *How can that be bad?*

They both were so lost in their thoughts they became complacent. A small group of furious Palace Guards caught them by surprise. Ten against two, they were bent on revenge, perhaps fearing what fate awaited them at the rebels' hands.

Kaushal tossed Tristan the Scimitar and swept one of the enemy off his feet, catching the lout's sword in midair. He had already considered the need to warn others not to wander alone through the castle complex and its environs. *So much for heeding my own advice!*

Some Guards had pistols. By trying to aim them in close quarters, pistols and severed hands went flying.

The floor became slippery with blood. Kaushal fell. He rolled aside as one soldier broke his sword on the stone where he had been. But he moved right into the path of another sword.

Tristan moved in front, took the hit, slipped, and fell. Kaushal dispatched that soldier and two more who hadn't fled. Kaushal touched his cheek and came away with blood.

The fight hadn't lasted long, but the loyalist Guards had come close to exacting revenge on the two rebel leaders.

He turned to Tristan who was lying face down.

"Don't die on me, old man," said Kaushal, helping him up. "We've been through too much for that to happen."

"I promise not to die," said Tristan, now standing, "but I might be in need of more than a tune-up."

Kaushal stared at his friend's innards. There were rubber tubes and cables, but his insides were mostly blinking electronic components and shiny mechanical parts.

"I'll be damned."

"That's not possible for a follower of the Way," said Tristan with a smile.

Part Eight

A New Era

It's unusual for these rogue worlds to overthrow their despotic regimes and join ITUIP, but it happens. Reclusive cultures often go into shock in the process, but that evolution seems inevitable. The more contact these cultures have with the remainder of the galaxy, the better off they are, at least economically. Many are also aberrations, so their citizens often benefit too.

—Swims-in-Rapids, University of New Haven Professor of Sociology (translated from buzzspeak)

Chapter Thirty-Eight

The Reluctant King

Anju walked behind Kaushal as he approached the dais where the throne sat. He stopped and dropped to one knee. She remained standing. Both were smiling.

The old priest with the wild, white hair held the Golden Scimitar high in both hands. He smiled at Kaushal but more or less ignored Anju. No one objected—that was tradition.

Finding a priest not involved in the First Pilgrim's and First Tribe's reign of terror hadn't been easy. Most from the Second Tribe had been beheaded; others were either banned or perished in dungeons. Pel, who seemed to know more about the history of Paradise and Eden than Tristan, had remembered a monastery located on a remote southern isle far from Angels' Bay, but still in the main archipelago. Novo, the leader of that sect, had reluctantly become the temporary First Pilgrim only after Pel promised the priest he could later return to his monkish ways.

Novo, born Franco Novo, had come from Paradise long ago with other refugees from the First Tribe. Gol Kovlyn had decided to save the order because it was popular with First Tribe nobles. Before the ice age on Paradise, the monks were known for their fine wines and ales, so important nobles had hoped they would continue producing them on Eden.

They had been censored, though, and banished to the Southlands. With the rise of Eden's Wilders, the monks there were largely forgotten, but not their products. They continued their traditional industry and became friendly with Wilders, who provided most raw materials and purchased much of their product, making what reached the capital much more expensive and sought after as luxury items.

In his short term as First Pilgrim, Novo's hair had become his trademark. People had a hard time understanding him—he spoke the old version of the First Tribe's dialect, mixed with influences from the Second Tribe. People wrote that off as Novo imbibing his monastery's product too often.

"Stand, Prince Kaushal." Kaushal rose. "I knew your father. He was a good man. May his guiding light shine on your reign." He handed Kaushal the Scimitar. "You are now King Kaushal, Eden's new ruler. I...." Novo swayed and seemed lost.

"The incense," said Anju from behind Kaushal, her voice a whisper.

There were some laughs from the nearest spectators.

"Yes, of course." Novo turned and received a smoking pot from an acolyte. The man's clothes had the permanent odor of ale-making materials, so the incense's odor helped cover that. Kaushal's nose was twitching from both as the priest started to chant and spread smoke about the hall.

"Let this ceremony be blessed by the Almighty Ra, his daughter Isis, and his son Osiris. Let us pray the Founder keeps us all safe during our lives and receives us warmly when we pass on to spend the rest of eternity in his grace. Blessed be the Almighty Ra. Long live King Kaushal."

The cheers made Kaushal blush.

***

"A pile of drax excrement," Kaushal later said to Kifi in the grand dining room. "I wish I could do away with all that mumbo-jumbo."

She put a hand on his cheek. "It will be an evolution. You need patience, my king. For now, it's something familiar for the people in this time of instability, something they can hold on to. Both First and Second Tribesmen take comfort in that."

"That will be my first edict: there will be no longer be First or Second Tribe, Mountain Folk or Wilders, loyalists or rebels. Only citizens of Eden."

"That sounds like a good first step," said Ezan, her mouth full of canapés and now with a patch over her empty eye socket. She examined another. "Anju told me you helped make these," she said in a mumble, "working through the night. Not bad. If you ever abdicate, you can be a baker. I'll be your best client."

"I learned how it's done when I worked in the kitchens. At least the theory. I was lucky they turned out well. I have a lot of friends there who helped."

"A man of many talents," said Pel, approaching their group with a large chalice filled with the best red wine from Novo's monastery. "Will you sing for us? Tristan says you have an excellent voice."

"How is he?" said Kaushal.

"Better. They're still doing some repairs on him aboard the ITUIP ship. He was already due for an overhaul. He sends you regards and regrets for not attending your coronation. You'll see him before we have to leave for New Haven."

"What will happen to you three?" said Kaushal.

"I'm expecting a reprimand for Kiana and me. Maybe community service. Because I want to swing by Sanctuary, where I spent many years, that won't be a problem, though. We can do our community service there."

"And Tristan?"

"He'll exploit a legal loophole in the Protocol. That was always the idea. That accord starts with the statement 'no living citizen of an ITUIP planet shall violate this Protocol on pain of punishment to be determined by the General Council.'"

"Why is that a legal loophole?" said Kifi.

Kaushal smiled; he had the answer to her question. "While I suppose ITUIP might consider Tristan a citizen, he isn't living in the biological sense." He winked at Pel. "Good show!"

"Thought you'd like that," said Pel. "He was the one who suggested taking advantage of the loophole in fact. He and others are advanced versions of androids now made in Earth's specialized factories. Tristan is number five. They are advanced mobile AIs in Human form, with emphasis on the I, which far exceeds ours, by the way, but I consider them to be unique sentient beings in our wonderful and diverse mix found among ITUIP worlds."

"Yes, he seems to be an able collaborator in whatever you do," said Kaushal.

"Kiana and I, well, we've always been something like rebels, always flaunting the rules." He looked across the hall. "And now I'd better go save her. She's drinking a little too much debating philosophy with old Novo, who likes wine as much as ale. We'll have to ready a platoon to carry him away from here. He won't stop otherwise."

***

Kaushal bid a bittersweet farewell to Kiana, Pel, and Tristan. The new king moped around for days afterwards, seeking refuge in the kitchens or in his songs for Anju.

"You have to snap out of your depression," said Anju one evening. "What in the name of the Founder is wrong with you, my king? We prevailed!"

Kaushal stared at her and frowned. "Just that. This whole role as king is an anti-climax. I never wanted to be king. I wanted revenge, and I wanted to save Eden from the First Pilgrim's tyranny. We did that, my love. Yes, we prevailed. But now what do I do? What do we do? Wander through this castle the rest of our lives solving the little problems of a peaceful people?"

"Soon traders will return. Eden will become a bustling planet. We have plenty to offer in trade for their technological wonders. We just have to develop our resources. That will be exciting."

"Let's hope that doesn't last too long. There's no reason we can't develop our own technology. Our people aren't stupid. We can send them to New Haven and other centers of learning, and they can return and build wonders themselves."

"That's what I like to hear. You'll be a steady, guiding hand for all that."

He frowned again. "There'll be other guiding hands. I'm not exceptional. This has to end now."

"Oh, please. You'll already be relinquishing much of your power to the People's Congress after elections are held. They'll still want you around, though. You're their hero. They need a hero now."

He sighed. "The true heroes are people like Kifi and Ezan, Kindri and Ravik, Chobi and Lakus, people who worked undercover and in impossible conditions to overthrow Gol Kovlyn. That's without mentioning all those who made the ultimate sacrifice."

"You're still the iconic symbol of that struggle. Pel told me what we did was unusual. These despotic regimes can endure for millennia, especially if they employ technological advances to keep people in their place."

Kaushal snapped his fingers. "That's it. I need to leave here and receive some guidance from Tristan, Pel, and others like them, and then go to work. Regimes like ours don't deserve to endure. I can work against them."

"And what about me?"

"Pel has a collaborator in Kiana. Won't you be mine?"

"Can we wait a few years at least? Until our children are grown?"

"Of course. But it will give me something more to wait for if I know I can make a difference out there." He gave her a kiss. "And we can do all that without me being king, my love. I want this monarchy to end as soon as possible. It's an anachronism. I don't care if people need it for a crutch. It's time they moved past it."

"Sounds like a plan," she said with a smile. "The Devil's in the details."

"No Devil, but we will have to work on the plan. And have patience."

"That last is my line," she said.

Chapter Thirty-Nine

Getting Down to Business

"Speaker Kaushal, the trade delegation's leader is here."

Kaushal nodded and closed his computer. He didn't have to suffer through too much pomp and circumstance as Speaker of the People's Congress, but greeting the leader of an important trade delegation was one example. The meeting was important because this first major trade agreement would now make ITUIP take notice of Eden.

Not long ago, a superstitious people would have taken H'bi Klaven as a monster or demon. His guest wasn't Human, but he represented a powerful consortium of traders from a small group of stellar systems. They were nearer Eden than most ITUIP worlds.

Kaushal made the ceremonial offering of his neck to the maw of the huge creature and stepped back. H'bi sat on his rump and rear legs and used the front legs to prop himself up. Arms started waving wildly as he went into a formal discourse about how glorious this day was, how they were looking forward to signing the agreement, and how wonderfully hospitable Eden's people were in their treatment of his delegation.

The AI eliminated most ceremonial fluff upon translation. It was now Kaushal's turn. His short speech was turned into a long discourse in H'bi's language. They then turned to serious negotiations.

***

"How'd it go?" Anju said to him when he met her for lunch at her lab in the outskirts of Angels' Bay.

Kaushal smiled. "H'bi thinks he's getting a good deal. I know we're getting a good deal. We are happy. ITUIP won't be. They wanted to deal directly with them. Now they'll have us in the middle. They're going to pay for having that quarantine on for so long. It still irks me that the Council didn't back my play on New Haven."

"I don't know. They were most likely impressed you persevered. And the Protocol's probably a good thing. It's a big galaxy. You never know which planets are going to go crazy. They're statistical outliers, of course, and mostly outside ITUIP, but these aberrations will occur."

"I'm just talking about our particular case." He bit into his pastry fold-over, a leftover from what he had cooked two nights ago. "I guess Pami arrived OK from her weekend off?"

Pami was Lakos' daughter who took care of their kids. She was with the children during the day and studied in Anju's institute at night. With Anju, she always had a tutor available. Kaushal's last decree as king was to end the practice of no schooling for female children. Before, only female children of the nobility had any schooling. Anju had pushed for that decree. Kaushal had backed her all the way. It made sense to give every citizen on Eden the chance to contribute.

The new law about schooling for all children was only one of many. The People's Congress had also passed laws to improve medical coverage, create veterans' benefits for those from both sides wounded in the battles for Eden, move toward a secular society that favored no religious belief or lack thereof, create local governments to handle local problems, and abolish all capital punishment, among many others. The pace was steady and measured; common sense and reason had won over raw emotion, although many members championed specific programs. Kaushal didn't know what to call it, but he liked what was happening.

"Pami is having trouble with geometry. We'll be working late tonight after she returns from classes."

"I can help there. I did well in geometry. My father tutored me."

"Do you miss him?"

"I remember him. What memories I have, I cherish." His eyes became moist as he held back tears. "I miss my mother more."

"Remember this: You couldn't have done what you did without them."

"You're becoming wise, old woman," he said, hugging her. "We're quite the team."

"But sometimes this half of the team has her work to do." She nodded toward her workbench. "I'm about to have a breakthrough in combining these circuits."

He gave her a kiss. "I'm back to my Speaker duties then. Maybe you can pick something up at Chobi's on the way home. Pami won't have time for cooking tonight, and I've already exhausted my list of recipes."

Epilogue

"You're a good fighter," said the burly man, jumping to his feet. He offered his hand to Kaushal. "Are you from the highlands?"

Kaushal rubbed his fist. The fellow had a steel jaw. He laughed but eyed others in the pub with concern. He knew the joke about the highlander meeting a gang of lowlanders. He didn't know there were two opposing lowland sides and said he belonged to the wrong one. Kaushal was sure he had the right group, though.

"You might say that. I need to talk to your leader."

Kaushal knew if the ruffian was the leader, he might be in trouble. But he guessed he wasn't because he had baited Kaushal. *All in good humor? Perhaps.*

Kaushal had spent seventeen standard days trying to infiltrate the opposition. It had been tricky avoiding the oppressive regime's Secret Police.

Another man scooted his chair back and stood. He was taller than the man Kaushal had decked. The thick, red beard and wild hair made him seem larger. Green eyes bore into Kaushal.

"I be that leader, stranger. What do you wish to discuss?"

"Not here," said Kaushal. "In private."

The first man glared at the second. "Why should we take any chances with this man-boy from the highlands?"

"Don't worry," said the second, "we can kill him later if needs be. Let's hear him out. But he's correct. Not here. Put the bag on him."

Three others grabbed Kaushal, tied his hands behind him, and put a rough cloth bag over his head. The first man whispered in his ear.

"You won't find any spies working for the Secret Police here. Outside, we have to be more careful. We'll guide you, but don't try to call to any friends who might not be our friends. Prepare yourself for a rough ride."

Kaushal smiled inside the bag and nodded. "Don't worry. I'm not with the Secret Police. I'm on your side."

He wasn't worried either. Pel's tracking device would tell his friends where he was. Anju, Kiana, or Pel would move in at the first sign of trouble. Once Kaushal won the opposition's confidence, he would bring them all in to help them destroy the regime.

***

Tristan awoke and stretched.

"We've updated everything," said the scientist. "You're good for another few hundred years if you stay out of trouble."

"His name should be Trouble. Hello, Tristan."

Tristan looked sideways and saw his friend Daneel. "I suppose they updated you too."

Daneel, the first high-performance android off the Earth assembly lines, smiled. "They're always tinkering. It's mostly software. You've found a special niche where you can be of service, my friend. I'm happy for you. And here I thought law enforcement was dangerous."

"Pel and friends are off to new adventures. I want to join them."

"I understand. They'll want you to spend a few more days here to make sure you're functioning properly, but no one will stop you from joining your new friends." He smiled.

"I learned something interesting the other day. Would you like to hear what I learned?"

"He asked about his name," said the scientist as he closed Tristan's chest. "Sometimes you fellows are just too damn curious. We pointed him to the sources. He received it well."

"When Humans first colonized Sanctuary, New Haven, and Novo Mondo," said Daneel, "they carried a digital record of all of Earth culture existing at the time of their departure with them. That was fortunate because they could eventually replace many works of art that were lost in the Tali invasion of Earth. In particular, digitized books. To make a long story short, our scientist friends here pointed me to some books in the old archives. I'm proud to say I'm named after a famous character in Earth fiction. I downloaded all the author's books. It's rather interesting that I was drawn to that character's same calling." He turned to the scientist. "It makes me suspect that you people programmed me that way. Was it on purpose or just playfulness?"

The scientist shrugged. "How would I know? All that happened well before I was born."

Note from Steve:

You have just finished the sci-fi saga, *Rogue Planet*. I know you have many available books nowadays to satisfy your reading appetite, so thank you for choosing this one. I hope you enjoyed it. I would greatly appreciate it if you post a review on Amazon and/or Goodreads so other readers and I can know what you liked and disliked and why. Yours might be one of the first! Also, please take a look at the following other sci-fi titles and stories set in the same fictional universe:

"The Chaos Chronicles Trilogy"

Survivors of the Chaos
Sing a Samba Galactica
Come Dance a Cumbia…with Stars in Your Hand!

Other books:

The Secret Lab (YA mystery)
Pasodobles in a Quantum Stringscape (contains Dr. Carlos stories)
Fantastic Encores! (contains stories involving characters from the trilogy plus more Dr. Carlos stories)

For more of my books—sci-fi, thrillers, and mysteries—visit my website: http:/stevenmmoore.com.
The above ebooks and other ebooks in my extensive catalog can be read for free in exchange for an honest review. Query me at steve@stevenmmoore.com.

In libris libertas....

Other titles by Steven M. Moore

"Detectives Chen and Castilblanco Series"

The Midas Bomb
Angels Need Not Apply
Teeter-Totter between Lust and Murder
Aristocrats and Assassins
The Collector
Family Affairs

The two detectives also appear in:

Pop Two Antacids and Have Some Java (short story collection)
The Golden Years of Virginia Morgan

Castilblanco's first case as an NYPD homicide detective can be found in:

World Enough and Crime (anthology with short stories from many authors)

A description of other e-books I've written can be found on my website: stevenmmoore dot com.

Want to see more Chen and Castilblanco mystery/suspense/thriller e-books? Drop me a line and tell me. I NEVER divulge email addresses!

Notes, Disclaimers, and Acknowledgements

Writing this novel was a lot of fun. Admittedly, it's a departure from my usual hard sci-fi and sci-fi thrillers. I don't read that much fantasy, but the books of John G. Stockmyer, like *Under the Stairs* and its sequels, convinced me that fantasy elements can be combined with good sci-fi. There's no magic here, other than that perceived by superstitious people—no dark forces, Jedi knights, or storm-troopers. But there are kings and queens, princes and princesses, mages (to borrow John's term), and religious fanatics. Even in ITUIP and its environs, Human societies can revert back to the Dark Ages. Any similarities to certain current earthly groups or societies can be considered intentional. Any similarities to existing persons are not.

I was a bit loose with all the religious mumbo-jumbo, especially with the influences of ancient Egypt. Ra, who later became Amun-Ra, was the top dog among Egyptian gods, but Isis and Osiris weren't his children. Nut, the sky wench, and Ra were actually enemies, and Nut was the mother of Osiris. And so forth. With the passing of centuries, it's no wonder the Founder as a teen got things confused. The confusion with Jewish-Christian-Muslim imagery was intentional too. If this bothers you, you've missed the point, and I'm sorry. This novel isn't about spirituality or religion— it's about the evil that can occur in the name of religion, perhaps a more futuristic and whimsical take on the same theme in *Soldiers of God*.

Freemasonry has been a mysterious and popular whipping boy in recent years; it also has many influences from ancient Egypt, but don't look there for influences here. Osiris and Isis are often referred to in Freemasonry, but the primary reference is to the polymath Imhotep, who wasn't a god. Over the centuries, we have seen many mishmashes of religions and religious symbolism. Unless you equate Tristan to Imhotep (not my intention, by any means), all the religious influences here are from past and current religions.

Imagine how all that religious heritage will evolve after Earth practically destroyed by the Tali (*Sing a Samba Galactica*) and mankind flees to the nearest stars. While some Humans might live for centuries (Pel and Kiana, for example), isolated groups of Humans will develop their own religions, myths, icons, and symbolism. My imagination can create one scenario—you're welcome to create your own.

Is the Way my version of the *Star Wars*' Force? Not at all. First, there's no dark side to the Way. Second, there's no magic in the Way. It's a philosophy, not a religion, with its genesis existing even before the Tali invasion among the riders of the big rigs, scientists, and other rugged individuals living outside Earth's political influence. It takes elements from many earthly religions…and others! It has evolved as Humans and their ET friends expanded through near-space, colonizing new planets and discovering old cultures. This imagined future-history is not a smooth one. Some things encountered in this expansion are dangerous.

The reader might think this novel is what *Star Wars* should be, but I've avoided borrowing ideas from my predecessors like *Star Wars* did, with its influence from certain Japanese Samurai movies, Edgar Rice Burroughs (the John Carter series), and Isaac Asimov (the Foundation trilogy)—except for the latter's Daneel Olivaw, of course, who I happily give a bow to. The true inspiration for this novel, though, is found in my Dr. Carlos stories. Carlos

Obregon was chief medical officer on the ITUIP exploratory starship *Brendan*. In his adventures, he had several close encounters with "rogue planets" and their regimes. In a sense, this novel is a huge elaboration on that theme.

All related Obregon tales and this one, though, have their ultimate origin in a what-if I noted many years ago after reading Charles Louis Fontenay's short story, "The Silk and a Song." In Charles's story, ETs enslave human beings. I asked myself at that time, "What if human beings on some backward planet are the bad guys and enslave other human beings?" This was long before our current oppressive theocracies appeared on the scene, but there were still plenty of others around. Unfortunately, we don't need to visit far-away planets to see that happening; it has occurred and now occurs right here on Earth.

This is the tale of one man's struggle to liberate his planet from an oppressive theocracy. Kaushal is a complex character. He's not perfect by any means. His intentions toward his people are good, though. He's also a charming cad at times too. Consider him the Arthur of the tale. His mysterious mentor, Tristan, plays the role of Merlin (although Mr. Dyson—see below—reminded me that there's a Tristan in the Arthurian legend). That famous sword in the Arthurian legend has its parallel in the Golden Scimitar. I'm not sure whether Kaushal or Tristan is the main character—they each give the other that honor. They're both important to the story. Of course, as often happens in an epic sci-fi fantasy, there are many characters in this novel, both good and bad. As in any revolution, there should be even more, but I had to keep the number reasonable. I also wanted no cliffhangers or the start of another trilogy.

In a very real sense, this is hard sci-fi, because there's no magic here. Better said, the only magic comes from present and future technologies. That's standard hard sci-fi fare. Clarke said, "Any sufficiently advanced technology is indistinguishable from magic." For retrograde Human societies, that would also be true. The First Pilgrim uses technology to become a mage and control Eden's citizens.

If you don't recognize the quotes from futuristic "historical figures" at the beginning of each part of the novel, that's because they're from ETs and Humans who played a role in ITUIP's history. I'll leave readers addicted to the entire series the puzzle of determining who Kiana and Pel really are. There are enough clues in the story to do so if you have read my other books. I'll be happy to see your guesses via email, if you're so inclined.

As a final note, I expect some sci-fi aficionados will object to the title. "Rogue planet" can mean a planet that escapes its solar system and wanders cold and lifeless among the stars. Here the term is only used as a planetary version of "rogue nation" as used by some glib politicians, in particular, George W. Bush, who put both Iran and North Korea in that category, for example. The ITUIP Protocol applied to Eden is a bit more imposing than what the U.S. applied to or is applying to either of those countries, of course.

As usual, my publishing team has done a remarkable job. Donna Carrick, a marvelous author in her own right, runs Carrick Publishing and does my formatting; the inimitable Sara Carrick always creates new and interesting cover art (the bad map of Eden is all mine); beta-readers Debby Kelly, Carol Shetler, and Scott Dyson (who's also an author of some excellent horror stories that go beyond my imagination's reaches to dark places where certain human psyches reside) look for logical errors that have escaped me and often find remaining editorial errors; and Amanda Kerr, of Bookbuzz.net, who ably lets the world know when I have a new book. These are all great people. Best of all, they are all internet friends whom I greatly value. This is an international team, by the way—the internet makes it a small world…and that's a good thing.

Steven M. Moore
Montclair, NJ
January 2016

About the Author

Steve has worked and lived in different parts of the U.S. and abroad. Born in California, he made his way to the Northeast of the U.S. by way of Colombia.

After teaching and doing research abroad and working in R&D in the Boston area, he decided to return to his first love, writing sci-fi, thrillers, and mysteries, where he uses those experiences with people, places, and science and technology to give life to his fiction.

He now is a full-time writer living with his wife in New Jersey. He has nineteen novels and three short story collections and also maintains an active blog where he comments on current events and posts book and movie reviews, interviews, short stories, and articles on writing fiction and the book business.

He loves to hear from readers. Contact him at steve@stevenmmoore.com.